THOROUGHLY
MANNERLY
MILLICENT

THOROUGHLY MANNERLY MILLICENT

•

Judi Thoman

AVALON BOOKS
NEW YORK

Published by Thomas Bouregy & Co., Inc.
160 Madison Avenue, New York, NY 10016

Library of Congress Cataloging-in-Publication Data

Thoman, Judi.
  Thoroughly mannerly Millicent / Judi Thoman.
      p. cm.
  ISBN 978-0-8034-9826-6 (hardcover : acid-free paper)
1. Scotland—History—19th century—Fiction.   I. Title.

  PS3620.H624T48 2007
  811'.6—dc22

                                          2006101342

PRINTED IN THE UNITED STATES OF AMERICA
ON ACID-FREE PAPER
BY HADDON CRAFTSMEN, BLOOMSBURG, PENNSYLVANIA

This is for the wee ones in my life; Andrew, Payton, Paige, and Parker. May you grow to love books. And for the ones gone from my life, but not forgotten.

Chapter One

Scotland 1873

Millicent had escaped! She'd fled the rigid constraints of London society on the wings of a promised oath of secrecy to her mother's editor. He'd facilitated her hasty departure and made her vow to never divulge a word of how she managed to leave the city. However, as her final destination drew near, she'd lost momentum. Mud seeped under the door of her hired carriage, and she felt trapped again. She could only imagine the reports of her demise posted in small print under the bold headlines of her famous mother's newly published book.

"Step aside," boomed an unfamiliar voice to rival the thunder rumbling through the mountains, and the clatter of rain upon her coach.

The open novel in her lap fell to the floor when she

recoiled in alarm. She peeked out of the worn curtain and jerked back against the lumpy seat.

A wraith!

Outside in the rain stood a specter of enormous proportions! The shadowy figure reminded her of the soulless monster, Frankenstein, in Mary Shelley's popular novel.

He loomed outside the carriage door. His black hooded cape flapped loudly like the wings of the angel of death. Millicent reached up with trembling fingers to extinguish her reading lamp, while she tried to still her labored breath and rompish heart.

"Unload these trunks." A harsh growl accompanied her apparition's demand. The heavy dialect of Scotland thick in his deep voice unsettled her and made words of wisdom from mother's book came to mind.

Nothing serves a man better than to give a good first impression by taking special care to temper his voice.

Millicent risked another peek. Would her trunks be plundered in search of riches? If recognized, would she be taken for ransom? She deserved as much. She deserved flaming coals heaped upon her. Millicent had placed herself in harm's way by traveling alone. She'd made a conscious choice to travel without a proper chaperone even knowing it would humiliate her mother and bring reproach upon the family name should she be discovered. She held both hands over her mouth for fear of making a noise to betray her presence.

A highlander! She'd expected to encounter highlanders in Scotland and even looked forward to it, since the Lord of McDougal Castle, her intended employer, was a highlander of sorts. But this . . .

"Do you have passengers inside?" the highlander demanded with churlish impatience. Her mother would disapprove. Millicent could not believe her misfortune to be stranded on an isolated road in the pouring rain and under attack. If his intent was dishonorable Millicent would be lost. If only she had not taken it upon herself to depart from London without revealing her whereabouts to someone she trusted.

"Only Lady Mary Wainright is inside." The coachman revealed her presence without the slightest twisting of his arm. Millicent recoiled at the words. Not only because she wanted to remain hidden. She hated to hear the man use the name which didn't belong to *her*. Millicent had taken her cousin's first name, and hoped not to be discovered.

"Please inform the lady I must lighten the carriage and need her to step down immediately."

It took only these words for Millicent to rally from her worry over damage to her possessions, to concern over what she perceived to be a personal attack. She considered her options and found she had none. Again words from her mother's book came to her.

In every matter, big or small, as far as it depends upon you, make the best of it. But how does one make the best of something like this?

"We have an umbrella ready for you, Lady Mary,"

the second coachman called out. "You must step down so the gentleman might fix the carriage."

"And you have gone over the edge," she mumbled to the coachman under her breath. What gentleman? It was obvious the coachmen now took their orders from the dark and probably evil highlander. Once she stepped from the carriage, she'd be at his mercy.

Millicent didn't have a choice. She opened the door and the biting rain pelted her. She pulled her hood lower. The coachman, true to his word, thrust her flimsy umbrella toward her for all the good it would do. In no time, her best traveling costume would be destroyed, but the highlander didn't seem to notice.

The wraith moved nearer to stand next to the broken wheel, which brought him closer to *her*. "Stand aside, Lady Mary. This will not be an easy task in the mire." He need not have issued the unnecessary order. Millicent had jumped back the second he'd moved closer to her.

He bent down to examine the wheel and made a rude noise. "Have you no lanterns to see by?"

At first Millicent imagined he spoke to her, and she started back toward the carriage where she still had a small amount of oil in her reading lamp. It hung from the side post, but perhaps it could be removed. There was another lantern on the opposite side she hadn't used at all.

"I said stand aside."

When the highlander barked at her a second time she

found it difficult not to snap back. Her fear receded and anger took its place. How dare he use that tone when she'd only intended to offer help?

One of the two coachmen stepped forward and nearly fell when he slipped in the mud. "Only the lanterns inside the carriage have oil. We've been fixing the wheel since first dark and have used up our allotment."

The highlander gave a rumbling growl and stopped to stare in Millicent's direction as if she'd somehow caused their plight. "Light those inside, please. Allow the door to hang open so I can see what I'm doing."

Millicent thought of her book resting on the floor of the carriage and sighed. She thought she might restore it with a bit of tender care, but any further abuse would more than likely make it impossible. Allow the doors to stand open indeed! At least she'd had the presence of mind to tuck her hatbox into the corner where it would not get rained upon too.

Once the coachman accomplished his task and light spilled out of the coach, Millicent heard the highlander groan. Startled, she turned back to see him staring at her. She took another step back into the shadows, so he wouldn't be tempted to continue his improper perusal.

She soon discovered from the vantage point she'd chosen she could assess *him* at her leisure without becoming obvious about it. She admitted her first impression of his voice had been colored by her vivid imagination. Under his Gaelic lilt, Millicent detected the cultivated tone of an educated man. If only he were not a giant perhaps she might even be grateful for his arrival.

His black cape now shone a deep green in the light filtering from the open carriage door. A tartan scarf hung over his left shoulder secured by a large silver buckle. The tartan was a similar deep green shot through with garnet red and gold.

The Scottish took pride in their ancestral colors, so more than likely he belonged to one of the many clans scattered about the highlands. His hat hid his face from her.

It occurred to Millicent, while the rain poured upon him, he gained nothing from attending to her stranded carriage. In truth, it seemed an act of heroism as she watched him tirelessly labor at the difficult task.

By the time the arduous chore was accomplished, the rain stopped. The clouds parted to bathe the coach in moonlight. Even as the darkness gave way to the prominence of the full moon, Millicent could see little of her rescuer's facial features.

"This repair should hold until you find someone to look after it properly. Your spare wheel is deplorable and not worth the trouble, however, I had no choice but to use it. How far do you travel before Lady Mary can rest and you can see to proper repairs?" the highlander asked.

One of the coachmen stepped forward to offer a rag. "Not far. Our destination is north to McDougal Castle."

The other hired man began to reload Millicent's

heavy trunks. "Thank you, milord, for all you have done. We will have someone look at the wheel there."

Millicent gulped. Why had the foolish coachman revealed her destination? And in the next instant, she castigated herself. Her rescuer had done nothing to make her think his intentions were anything other than honorable. Her unease came from her own deception. She had no one to blame but herself. Millicent chose to escape to the highlands rather than face her own mother.

The highlander took the rag and wiped his hands. "Why did you choose this road? You have traveled farther than necessary by coming this way. You will find a better road ahead to your right."

He turned to face Millicent for the first time. The moon over his shoulder left his face in the shadows. "My lady, I apologize for your discomfort. I should not have asked you to step out of the carriage." He gave a brief bow and then turned back to the coachmen without giving her a chance to speak or even offer thanks. Why hadn't she spoken sooner? What happened to her tongue?

"See Lady Mary safely inside and pray she does not come to harm for this soaking she's had to endure. You should have known better than to come this way and bear heavy responsibility for choosing this road."

The tall, dark, and mysterious highlander championed her interests. Millicent raised her foot and tried to determine the best pathway through the thick river of mud trailing back to the carriage door.

"Take care, my lady," the highlander said in a more gentle tone. He swept his plaid scarf from his shoulder, outstretching it upon the muddy ground at her feet.

Millicent wanted to protest. But before she recovered enough aplomb to offer her heartfelt appreciation of his gallant gesture, he swung up onto the back of his fretful steed and bolted away. Once secure in her carriage, she watched him racing in the moonlight around Loch Droma.

"Oh my," she gasped as the beat of her heart increased even more than earlier when she'd been in fear of her life. How curious. "Please fetch the gentleman's scarf in case I ever have occasion to return it to him," she told the coachman before they continued their journey.

By the time the sun began to rise over the moors, in Millicent's highly imaginative mind, the highlander became the most handsome man to walk the earth. As she looked at the muddied scarf on the carriage floor next to her feet, she wondered if she would have the opportunity to return it and thank him properly. It was the least she could do.

"We will arrive shortly. McDougal Castle is close." The coachman's herald made her move to the window. She drew back the curtain. The sun had begun its ascent over the lowland to her left and a mountain loomed high in front of them.

Millicent's spirit would not be dampened with the onset of yet another rain shower. Every turn of the carriage wheels brought Millicent to the rationalization that she had made the right decision to escape the comforts of London for this untamed land.

No regrets.

No recriminations.

Until.

At the sight of her intended destination, McDougal Castle, her courage wavered once again. In the center of a green oasis, on the top of a steep hill, stood a monstrosity fit for lightning and peals of thunder as steady companions.

Without sufficient sleep and still sodden from hem to waist, she hoped to blame her sorry state of mind for the images conjured by McDougal Castle. Indeed, as they drew nearer, the castle seemed more likable. Aside from the original main hall, Millicent counted six protruding additions of varying size and character. Their styles ranged from darkly whimsical to bizarrely gothic.

The rows of tiny rock cottages with thickly thatched roofs at the foot of the steep hill were infinitely more inviting. The smoke from their cozy peat fires curled into the rain-saturated dawn to welcome her.

Once situated inside the castle hall, Millicent truly grew faint of heart. Nothing seemed warm and inviting about the great stone galley. Its walls were covered with all manner of aged weaponry, each more than likely bearing a tale she hoped never to hear told. Nor had the servant who showed her inside welcomed her. So little light shone from the fireplace at the end of the room,

Millicent needed to take extraordinary care not to make a misstep in the dark.

"I see we have company at the break of dawn," came a woman's Scottish brogue from behind her. Millicent shifted to see a rotund figure emerge from the shadows.

Millicent understood how inappropriate it was to arrive unheralded at such an extraordinary hour of the morning. "I am Lady Mary Wainright, from London for the position of governess." Millicent sat her precious hatbox upon the floor next to her shamefully muddy feet and pulled a sealed envelope from the valise at her wrist.

"Mrs. McDuffy. I'm the housekeeper here." The older woman stared at the envelope Millicent held toward her as if uncertain what to do with it.

Millicent extended her reach with the letter. "This is my letter of introduction and recommendation for the position of governess."

The housekeeper gingerly received the envelope.

With her hands free, Millicent began to remove her kid gloves.

"A paper to recommend you?" Mrs. McDuffy asked. She stared at the letter with suspicion before depositing it into one of long pockets on her apron.

"I'm certain the position requires it," Millicent suggested. "Would you rather I gave it to His Lordship myself? I suppose I might be forgiven a small breach of etiquette." Her mother instilled in her the knowledge that good breeding was not just formalistic rituals, but respectful behavior designed to make others feel at ease. If for whatever reason her letter worried the housekeeper, Millicent would gladly accept the responsibility of seeing it safely in the hands of the master of the house.

Mrs. McDuffy gave a tenuous smile but didn't return the note. "I will give it to His Lordship when he returns. This way, then, to your rooms."

Millicent followed the housekeeper, taking caution not to jostle her hatbox. She was ushered across the length of the room and into one of the later additions. Cold gray stone gave way to wood and richly colored tapestry-covered walls. The ceilings were low enough to keep the heat where one might have occasion to feel the warmth.

The housekeeper seemed in a quandary about where to place her. They walked through four different wings before they settled upon what the housekeeper dubbed to be suitable rooms for the *proper* English governess.

"Aye, this will suit you fine," the woman said with a thin smile. "You are younger than the other two ladies who have come to apply for the position."

Millicent almost failed to hide her surprise. *Two* other women had come to apply? She hadn't considered she might not be the only one. How foolish of her. "*Three* women are seeking the same position?"

"Aye. His Lordship needs help wi' the children soon. He is very worried about the babes as you will see for yourself. He married too young and then was left wi' wee babes when his poor wife died. He's only a score and nine. You shall meet Lord McDougal this evening along wi' the other women."

"Thank you, Mrs. McDuffy. I will entertain myself until the dinner hour arrives by gathering the sleep I lost on the road over Loch Droma."

The housekeeper nodded and turned to go, but hesitated in the doorway. "I will send a tray to your room to break your fast, and tea is at the usual time. We meet in the dining room after the sound of the second gong for the evening meal. Everyone will want to meet wi' you. The children have already become acquainted wi' both Miss Sully and Miss Carter. We hadna' expected a lady of quality to apply here in the highlands."

"It's uncommon, but sometimes even titled ladies must make a living if they choose not to be a burden upon their families." Millicent couldn't meet the woman's eyes while she used her free hand to tug at the snaps on her wet coat. Her ruse was already more difficult than she'd imagined. Titled ladies rarely sought positions unless the family was in dire straits, and she hadn't thought the housekeeper would challenge her ruse.

The housekeeper smiled warmly. "I shall send a man up wi' your trunks."

Millicent gave a more formal curtsy. "Thank you. Your kindness is much appreciated."

Even though the sun streamed through the numerous oriel windows, Millicent decided to rest. She'd need her wits about her if she'd be able to pull this deception off. She locked the inner door to the second room with her bed. As she moved past a marqueterie chest with a bronze statue of cupid, she absentmindedly laid her gloves on the marbled top.

Anxious to be relieved of her heavy burden, she placed her hatbox on the end of the bed, opened the lid and peered inside. "We have finally arrived at our new home, Aphrodite. My precious, now you can stretch out next to me on the bed to finish your sleep."

Millicent extracted the huge mound of fluffy white fur and sat her pet upon the bed. Pale blue eyes blinked up at her for only a moment then closed again. Aphrodite rolled into a ball. She purred so loudly Millicent tucked her under the covers to mute the sound. Millicent then hurriedly removed her wet clothes, her ruined slippers, and then bathed her muddied feet in the wash basin. Not having slept the entire night, she needed just a short nap and perhaps a dream of a handsome highlander.

Chapter Two

The sound of a childish giggle interrupted Millicent's restful dream of walking in the clouds. She struggled awake to hear the sound more clearly defined. However, when Millicent opened her eyes, no child was in sight. She pulled up to lean back upon her elbows and discovered something cold and wet about her feet.

At the same time, a young boy popped up at the side of her bed and startled Millicent. He held a silver tray of scones in his hands. A sprite of a girl, not much taller, sprouted up next to him and pulled the tray away from him.

"Scones, miss?" the sprite said. "Left over from tea."

Both broke into another fit of giggles. Millicent looked down to her bare feet, the covers carefully folded back to display them. Exposing her naked feet to anyone was not a small matter but Millicent decided to let it pass for the moment. The thick clotted cream slathered over her toes was another matter altogether.

"Scones?" Millicent questioned, taking care not to show irritation in her voice. She'd learned long ago from her brothers never to startle to the point of uttering an exclamation or allowing it to show on her face. "And this is the way your father has trained you to serve them to guests in his house?"

Both children nodded and smiled but the glint of mischief in the girl's pale golden eyes told Millicent a tale on its own. These children did not want a governess interfering in their lives. They had covered Millicent's toes with clotted cream to get rid of her.

Millicent held her hand toward the tray and took a scone. A flash of surprise crossed the girl's intelligent, pixie-like face. Millicent broke off a piece and reached the morsel down to her well-slathered toes. Without hesitation, she swiped the piece of scone across the top of her foot and captured a liberal serving of cream. When Millicent popped it into her mouth, both children appeared repulsed.

"Would you like a bite?" Millicent asked as she broke off another small piece of the scone and started to stretch downward again. Millicent was the only girl in a family with five older brothers, who each took delight in tormenting her in their own unique way. These small children had another thing coming if they thought they could best her with this ploy.

When the boy cautiously reached out his hand to accept Millicent's offer, his sister grabbed him and jerked him aside. At precisely this moment, Aphrodite awakened and decided to investigate the commotion. Still under the blankets, she moved toward Millicent's feet.

"Would you care to pet my aardvark?" Millicent pointed to the large moving lump. Aphrodite was entirely too large for a housecat and made an imposing aardvark under the covers.

The boy's eyes widened, but he nodded eagerly. His sister allowed a sharp hiss to escape from between her teeth. "Come Bryon." The girl set her tray on the edge of the bed and took a step back.

"I want to pet an ourvark."

Millicent was about to correct him when his sister dragged him by the back of the collar from the room, mumbling all the while under her breath about aardvarks and such, whatever they might be.

So, these were the children Millicent had come to oversee. It was evident they had no desire for a governess and were willing to take whatever measures necessary to make certain no one accepted the position.

Millicent found it amusing. It would be a personal challenge to succeed where the other women might fail. Had the others been treated to the same welcome as she?

Not for the first time since her arrival, her scheme to come to the highlands pricked her conscience.

Perhaps her conscience wouldn't trouble her if she

could be a true help to this family. How badly it would go for the children once they were grown and sent off into the world if they failed to respect society's dictates. Millicent could attest firsthand to the pariah effect settled upon a person with poor manners.

Even an individual who took extraordinary care to uphold proper decorum found it difficult to maintain the necessary propriety at all times. Who could know when an unrestricted sneeze might become a disruptive occasion for embarrassment? Or the elbow she placed firmly in Lord Finch's ribs would cause such concern to her mother's friends? Or a dance instructor would tell everyone who cared for idle gossip that Millicent could not keep step with the late dances. Hopefully, she wouldn't be expected to know *Scottish* dance steps. The list of Millicent's transgressions seemed endless despite all of her diplomatic mother's tireless lessons.

The sound of the gong startled Millicent for the second time and the children's words about tea time sunk into her sleep-clogged brain. Somehow, Millicent had slept the entire day away. Never mind she'd not slept the previous night, what would they think? She hated for the first impression of her to be a layabout. She jumped from her bed and threw a blanket around her before she looked into the next room for her trunks. Without time to waste, she picked the first day dress she found. It was a modest, fawn wool garment, which would neither be ostentatious or too plain.

In truth, she had no idea what costume a governess

might wear in the highlands. She'd hoped manners, fancy dresses, and all things considered proper English could be dismissed in highland society.

In the household where Millicent grew up, the governess was treated as a member of the family. But Weatherly Manor was not a typical household in any respect.

The family wealth was renowned in all of England. It was that same wealth which troubled Millicent to no end. What gentleman would choose her without giving undue attention to the exorbitant dowry settled on her? It seemed impossible to believe the money wouldn't take preference. Because of her dowry, for the previous two years she'd cried off when time came for her to be launched.

The gossipmongers called her peculiar, but still there were numerous offers for her hand. And *some* she might have even considered if not for the worry her money was infinitely more attractive than she. Several even proclaimed their love, however Millicent couldn't return the feigned sentiment.

In the desolate highlands and masked under the assumed identity of her own dear cousin, Mary, she would be able to avoid the nonsense altogether. Let people call her peculiar and whisper behind her back. Here in the highlands, she wouldn't be a humiliation to anyone, save herself.

Millicent hurried to find a servant who could direct

her to the dining room before she made a late entrance and rudely kept everyone waiting.

Only the housekeeper was waiting, and showed Millicent to her seat and went about her business.

"Thank you," Millicent called as the woman rushed away. They evidently didn't cling to ceremony at McDougal Castle.

Millicent took the time alone to grow accustomed to her surroundings. The long table had been set for a small party of diners. The warm and inviting brightly papered walls cheered her. At the far end of the room, the remnant of the setting sun filtered through a stained glass window emblazoned with the family crest. All in all, if the room reflected the family, Millicent took heart.

Millicent had started to relax, until a table underneath the stain glass window caught her attention. The table was adorned in plaid—a very familiar tartan pattern of deep green and garnet red.

She wished to draw nearer for a closer look but even from where she stood there could be no mistaking the plaid.

Could her highlander be employed by the McDougal clan? Or perhaps even be a member of the family? Maybe a cousin of Lord McDougal? Again, she tried to imagine his face.

Millicent was about to silently chastise herself for not properly employing her thoughts when two women entered the room together followed by the housekeeper.

Mrs. McDuffy went about lighting the candles until she remembered to make the introductions. "This is Miss Carter." At the sound of her name, the tallest woman gave a slight curtsy to Millicent.

"And this is Miss Sully."

Miss Sully met Millicent's eyes for the briefest time before she looked down to the floor. Like the first woman introduced, she gave a polite curtsy.

"Ladies, this is the third and I believe the last person to join us. Allow me to introduce you to Lady Wainright."

Millicent curtsied and tried not to wince at the housekeeper's words. Even her wayward brothers had never called her Lady Wainright. That particular appellation was reserved for a widowed aunt. So began her formal foray into a life of dishonesty. Not to mention the fact the name Lady Millicent was the legal title conferred on her at birth and, as such, shouldn't be altered even slightly as dictated by decorum.

"Please call me Lady Mary. Lady Wainright is an aunt, once married to my deceased uncle, Lord Carlton Wainright."

At the declaration of Millicent's title, the women appeared uneasy as they all took their seats. Miss Carter's face turned gray and Miss Sully hung her head so low, Millicent couldn't see her expression at all.

"*Lady* Mary?" Miss Carter said. "Are you related to the Duke and Duchess of Weatherly?"

Millicent settled into her chair and tried to prepare

herself for the half-truths she was about to speak. She needed all her wits. "Yes, I am. It's a very large family. The long deceased Duke of Weatherly, my grandfather, had seven brothers. Each of those brothers had many offspring, most of them of the male persuasion. There are so many of us, it's hard to keep an accurate account. We are much like a small town when we all get together." Everything Millicent said was true. So far.

A frown furrowed Miss Carter's otherwise pleasant face. "You are very young, Lady Mary. Why would someone of such a tender age and from a distinguished lineage travel this far for a position as a governess?"

Once she asked the personal question, Miss Carter gasped and covered her mouth with both hands. Her soft brown eyes blinked as if to hold off tears. "Forgive my rudeness. It's just I can't possibly have a chance to gainsay you for the position with your unique qualifications."

Any indication of malice in the woman's words didn't exist. Millicent could easily understand why Miss Carter would wonder. "While my aunt, the current Duchess of Weatherly, is celebrated at court and among polite society, not all of our family enjoys the same wealth and privilege." Again, Millicent managed to refrain from an untruth. "Sadly, the estate struggles to sustain so many mouths as the Wainright men have produced."

Millicent never understood the inequity. Her father as eldest son received the lion's share of the entailed estates. The other brothers, her uncles, were not nearly so fortunate. And it would be the same for her five brothers. Her eldest brother, Andrew would inherit not only the title, but most of the land and income it produced while the others would be left to their own devices and a yearly allowance that only seemed to dwindle with each passing generation.

Millicent tried not to grimace. Telling a lie was so much harder in practice than in theory. Her conscience protruded much like a sharp needle straight into her heart.

"My mother and I have always depended upon the charity of my father's family. While I probably could have taken a position among them, I wished to make my own mark on the world, even though it is not commonplace for me to choose to do so." Millicent had tried to speak slowly, but by the end of her speech she couldn't breathe and needed to rush.

Miss Carter's face was pinched. "How noble of you."

Millicent couldn't detect a hint of sarcasm in the woman's tone and felt mortified about her ghastly lie.

"I think so too." The admiration in Miss Sully's voice nearly undid Millicent. She looked down to where she twisted her napkin in her lap. Why did she think she could do this? Why hadn't she given it more thought?

It was almost more than Millicent could bear. Her mother always said to ignore the vigilance of one's conscience was a serious transgression. It showed a lack of moral character which could lead to unknown horrors. She stared down at the emerald ring given to her more than two years prior on her seventeenth birthday along with her hateful dowry and fought the urge to flee that very moment.

When the housekeeper ushered the children to the table, the distraction gave Millicent a chance to calm her fraying nerves. Perhaps the first falsehood would be the hardest? She could only hope so.

The almost tidy children hardly resembled the rough and hoyden who'd earlier endeavored to terrorize her. The girl's pale blond locks struggled against the bonds of a pink bow, twice as wide as her head. The bow greatly clashed with the orange frock with lime-green vertical stripes. The look of defiance on such a petite and fragile face made Millicent sad. She much preferred mischievousness.

Although considerably younger, the boy stood nearly as tall as his sister. His auburn hair and golden eyes, fringed with long dark lashes would easily captivate attention. Even in his youth, he promised to become an exceptional looking man. The expressive twinkle in his amber eyes reminded Millicent of a tabby cat she'd once rescued from an alley. A very ornery cat, which made her dear Aphrodite both nervous and cranky.

The housekeeper properly introduced the children and bade them in a stern tone to mind their manners. When a look passed between them, Millicent wondered if trouble might be looming, despite the dire warning.

His Lordship's daughter, Caitlyn, frowned from the moment she sat down. "My name is Caitlyn McDougal." The young girl spoke too loudly and with authority as if she had not heard the housekeeper tell everyone her name only seconds before.

"My brother is Bryon McDougal. He is only *six*, but he is sound of mind. He is very brave and so am I. The highlands are our home!" Caitlyn's voice escalated in volume until she nearly screamed.

A battle cry!

Millicent was certain of it. This rompish girl intended to gain their attention and it more than likely could end unpleasantly for all those present at His Lordship's table.

"He is very big for six." Caitlyn stood again before she continued, but the effect made little difference due to her short stature in comparison to the table. "We do not need a governess."

Miss Sully sharply inhaled. Miss Carter glared at the loud and rebellious girl.

War had been declared. Millicent hid the beginnings of a smile behind her hand and prayed it wouldn't be noticed. It could make matters worse if Caitlyn didn't believe she was taken seriously.

"How old are *you*, Miss Caitlyn?" Millicent hoped to distract her.

"I am nine and soon will be ten years of age. I can govern myself and Bryon as well. We already have a nursemaid, if that is not bad enough." Caitlyn snorted her disdain.

Bryon nodded at his sister's words with approval on his worshipful young face.

"If we had a mother, we wouldn't need a governess," Caitlyn said, and stomped her small foot for emphasis. Despite the girl's deplorable manners, Millicent appreciated Caitlyn's emotional pain buried beneath the prickly nettles of her ill-mannered words.

"Do you like frogs?" Bryon asked Millicent. "Or only *ourvarks?*

"Aardvarks," Caitlyn corrected. "Remember we saw a picture of one in the great book from Papa's study." She turned to Millicent and rudely pointed her small finger. "You lied."

Her words shocked Millicent to the core. How had the child of all people discovered her secret?

"You don't have an aardvark," Caitlyn said.

"Do you like frogs?" Bryon interrupted his sister and stared at Millicent.

She wondered if he intended to show a pet frog at the table along with the shirred eggs Millicent had never seen served so late in the day.

"I've never met a frog I disliked." Millicent tried to remain unruffled but when Caitlyn accused her of falsehood she had almost blurted a confession.

Miss Sully suddenly perked up. "I like frogs. Very much so."

Millicent was surprised and grateful to have someone else join the conversation. However, she didn't anticipate it would be shy Miss Sully.

"How about mice?" Caitlyn asked. The girl reached under the table and pulled up a burlap bag. She plopped in onto the table and pulled the drawstring. Five tiny gray mice scurried out of the tattered bag and took off in every direction at a speed much faster than the human eye.

Both Misses Sully and Carter began to scream at the same time. Miss Sully jumped onto her chair while Miss Carter sprang from hers and ran from the room. Her screams echoed down the hallway as she made her retreat.

Although it took courage, Millicent didn't move from her place. When one of the baby mice crawled up onto her plate, stopped and then stood on its hind feet to sniff the air, she stayed the course.

The serving staff didn't help at all. The parlor maid screamed and ran off shortly after Miss Carter departed. The butler didn't appear any happier to contend with mice upon the table, but at least he didn't flee. Instead, he wrung his hands and moaned.

"To the nursery!" a voice boomed directly over Millicent's shoulder. The noise nearly deafened her. Both children flinched at the sound before they bolted from the room without uttering a solitary word of protest.

A lumbering, red-headed giant of a man moved into Millicent's line of sight. "The wee ones have spirit."

Millicent wasn't certain if he meant the wee children or the wee mice still at large.

When he laid his hand onto the table and the nearest mouse climbed onto the mountain with fingers, Millicent was certain her eyes were as big as the saucer under her teacup.

He shot her a sidelong look and grinned. "You dinna allow a wee mouse to scare you?" He spoke with a strong accent which had a familiar ring about it. For a second Millicent wondered if he might be her highlander. Wouldn't he say something about his gallant moonlight rescue if he were one and the same?

He raised his hand with the mouse cradled in the center of his palm and offered it to her. Did he mean for her to hold it? Millicent fought the urge to pull back.

As he held the mouse in front of her face, Millicent got a closer view—too close. The tiny whiskered creature almost looked offended because she hesitated to pet it. Miss Sully climbed down from her perch upon the chair and moved nearer to see.

"Are they yours?" Miss Sully asked.

"These wee ones came to live in my clothes drawer after they lost their mother to the *cat*." He spit the word cat.

Millicent nearly succumbed to a fit of giggles as she watched the giant's face soften as he spoke of the mice. It was then Millicent noticed his eyes. The golden eyes resembled young Bryon's. He must be related to the children.

"So you've become their mother?" she asked.

At first, he seemed taken aback by her outspokenness before he grinned sheepishly. "Aye, I have."

Just as quickly, his smile hardened into a menacing frown. "If I find my wee ones gone from their wee nestie again, I will flay whoever dares to disturb them."

The sound of pattering feet in the hallway told Millicent his intended audience heard him and ran away in fear.

When Miss Sully reached a trembling hand toward the baby mouse, Millicent had newfound admiration for her.

"You'll be very careful, Miss?"

"I've always wondered how it would feel . . ." Miss Sully touched the back of the mouse with the tip of her index finger.

"Braw lassie," he said and placed it into her cupped and trembling hand.

"After my father died, I couldn't have a pet. My mother said she could only worry about food to feed her children and a pet would be beyond the pale."

The man looked ready to cry for her. Millicent chewed her lip as she worried about what her presence might mean for this poor, sweet woman.

"I vow to make this right," Millicent said as much to herself as anyone else.

"Make what right?" Miss Sully asked. "I am fine now. Would you like a turn?"

Millicent shuddered. "If you always wanted a pet,

you should have one," she blurted when she could think of nothing else to make sense.

"Lady Mary, are you all right?" Miss Sully asked. "I assure you I've not suffered greatly for the lack of a pet. How kind of you to worry about me."

"Would you be wantin' a wee mouse?" the grinning giant asked Miss Sully.

Millicent couldn't be certain, but it was entirely possible she'd made the biggest mistake of her life by coming to the highlands. Now how to make it right?

Chapter Three

Because of the children's behavior the previous evening, the entire household feared what the children next intended. Millicent's stomach complained for a long overdue repast.

The morning meal fared badly. Interruptions with all manner of complaints stopped most of the food before it even reached the table. Only weak tea and toast were on the sideboard. Even as hard as she tried, Mrs. McDuffy couldn't persuade the cook from her sickbed.

While Millicent understood and commiserated with the serving staff, when first the evening and then the morning meal went missing so did the good humor of all in McDougal Castle.

When the gong finally sounded for tea, she breathed a sigh of relief.

"Lady Mary, it's good to see you so cheery after our trial last eve and then again this morning," Miss Sully said when they all took their seats in the dining room.

Millicent didn't feel cheery, not in the least. In point of fact, Miss Sully appeared to be the one energized by the events. Poor Miss Carter seemed ready to bolt at any second.

"Does anyone know if Lord McDougal be joining us soon?" Millicent wondered aloud.

Caitlyn arrived and took the seat at the head of the table in His Lordship's chair which seemed to swallow her. Once again, her action showed her attempt to take control. For one so young, it truly was precocious. "Papa is still away, but Mrs. McDuffy says he could be home at any time."

Millicent smiled in an attempt to ward off any further demonstrations. "I'm certain you miss him very much while he is away."

"I miss Papa even when he is at home," Bryon said as he took a seat next to Millicent.

"He's very young," Caitlyn said and pointed to her brother. "But he is strong and listens well to what I say to him."

"That is wise of him." Millicent meant it. In Caitlyn's current agitated state she might not take kindly if he disobeyed her.

Caitlyn eventually nodded. "I will be ten on my next birthday. Then I shall have my own horse. A very big one."

"How wonderful for you." Millicent took two large scones as the tray was passed by the parlor maid. "I was ten before I was allowed to ride even a small pony."

"Neither Miss Carter nor Miss Sully ride." Caitlyn jerked her little chin toward the women, more than likely disturbed by the idea.

"I think perhaps Miss Carter and Miss Sully have other interests to occupy them." Uneasy for the tender feelings of both of the other women, Millicent didn't care for the direction of the conversation.

"Horses are smelly and dangerous." Miss Carter spoke for the first time, only to make Millicent wish she had remained silent. Miss Sully had the good sense not to say anything to incite Caitlyn to action.

Millicent wondered if the women did not understand they were undergoing trial by fire. Every word they uttered would be weighed and measured by the children of Lord McDougal.

"I do not want a governess who thinks horses are smelly," Caitlyn said speaking too loudly again.

Miss Carter inclined her head in a half-nod and gave Caitlyn a thin smile. "I am well aware, Miss Caitlyn, of how well you dislike what I have said. Nevertheless, as far as it depends on my sensibility, I will not misrepresent myself to you. Even to gain a position I need desperately."

With that, tears started to sting the back of Millicent's eyes. She was a veritable dung-heap of deceit. She opened her mouth to speak, but couldn't. How would it reflect on her mother if she admitted she'd already told a boldfaced lie to gain a position she didn't deserve?

Millicent hid her grimace behind her hand until she gained control. Something needed to be done to right the situation. "I believe Miss Carter and Miss Sully represent most of polite society. There are, of course, some ladies who find riding amusing, but the vast majority do not. My own aunt, the Duchess of Weatherly has never ridden upon the back of a horse. She finds no interest in them at all, other than to pull her carriages. In recent years, riding has grown more popular among the younger set, but many say it is a passing fancy."

"Thank you, Lady Mary," Miss Sully said. "I always wished to have an opportunity to ride."

"I wouldn't want to go where women don't ride." Caitlyn stood and pounded her small fist on the table. "I won't go to London. Ever. I won't."

"You missed my point, Miss Caitlyn," Millicent said, taking care to keep her tone mild. "Ride or do not ride. Each person should feel free to make their choice without fear others view their preference as inappropriate. Some people, like Miss Sully or Miss Carter, have not made their choice based on their own free will. Perhaps they did not have the resources made available for them to ride for leisure sake."

Caitlyn thrust her chin higher. Millicent decided to change her tactics. "Perhaps there are children in the village who would like to have a horse to ride, but it is beyond their means."

"Do you like frogs?" After his too familiar question Bryon stuffed an entire scone into his mouth.

"Not now," Caitlyn said to her brother, and then waved her hand in a dismissive manner. Her tone told Millicent she was unhappy to be corrected in front of everyone. Millicent understood that well enough. However, it wouldn't have been fair to the other women if Millicent hadn't spoken on their behalf.

"I thought we talked of frogs last evening," Millicent reminded Bryon. "Perhaps it slipped your mind?"

Miss Sully gently cleared her throat. "I once saw an interesting frog with tiny sharp teeth."

"Where?" Crumbs flew from Bryon's mouth when he spoke.

"At the zoological society in London," Miss Sully said with awe. "It is heaven on earth."

Bryon swallowed his food with a loud gulp. "I want to see a frog with sharp teeth. Did you stick your fingers in its mouth? Did it look as big as this one?" He ducked his head under the table before he brought both hands over his plate. Between them was the largest bullfrog Millicent had ever seen.

Once Bryon removed his hands, the creature leaped high into the air. When it landed with a plop into a bowl of clotted cream in front of Miss Carter, she screamed so loudly she frightened the frog. To show its displeasure, the frog began to jump erratically back and forth and to and fro. In a short order of time, the frog's impressively quick feet had explored almost every inch of the table. All the while, it vocally croaked its irritation, which only made Miss Carter scream all the more loudly before she cried off and dashed from the room.

Millicent sighed. She understood Miss Carter's frustration but she was famished. At this rate the children would win the battle easily.

The servants came out in full force to set to rights the disrupted household. However, all of the clumsy hands diving about only added to the confusion as the bullfrog continued to elude them.

Bryon laughed loudly and encouraged his frog. "Go, Goliath, go!"

When Goliath settled upon a heaping pile of kidneys, Miss Sully showed her true mettle. She captured the frog between her small hands and crushed it to her chest. Goliath at first seemed annoyed and wiggled against her, but soon seemed to understand she would not be deterred. Goliath allowed his long greenish-brown legs to relax down to Miss Sully's waist.

"To the nursery!" Both Bryon and Caitlyn appeared impressed with Miss Sully's catch. However, neither had time to offer congratulations before the booming voice of the giant brought the frog's adventure to an abrupt end.

He shouted so loudly, Millicent swore she saw the chandelier above their heads sway from the percussion of his massive voice.

Both children bolted from their chairs and streaked out the door. Whoever the red-haired giant was, he had the respect and fear of the McDougal offspring.

This time the housekeeper came to issue a proper introduction to the unnamed man. "Lady Mary and Miss Sully, allow me to introduce Lord McDougal's younger brother, Lord Fen."

Millicent's curiosity would not be contained. "Lord Fen, did you recently mend a wheel on the back road to McDougal Castle?"

"Nay, I have been too busy with my brother's children to venture far. The wee ones are trying to scare you." He reached for the bullfrog still nestled against Miss Sully's chest, but then drew his hands back as if he thought better of it. By now the bullfrog looked positively smug at its improved situation in life.

"It would seem Miss Sully is now the forerunner in the race for governess." Lord Fen sounded proud of her accomplishment as if he'd had something to do with it.

Millicent was rooting for Miss Sully as well. Any woman who could catch a frog should not be taken lightly. Millicent's own niece had a penchant for anything green and living.

A thought occurred to Millicent. "Since we can no longer have our tea *here*, perhaps I might convince the housekeeper to send a tray for us to my room. Will you join me, Miss Sully? Please?"

For a second, Miss Sully looked ready to decline until Lord Fen managed to wrangle the frog from her hands in a decent enough approach and sent it off with another servant.

The poor woman then ran her hands down the front of her dress. The frog had managed to transfer a great deal of their uneaten lunch onto Miss Sully. "I need to tend to my soiled garment. I only have one dress for daytime and one for evening and of course one for church."

Miss Sully still had not said she'd come. But then she smiled and shrugged. "I'll find Miss Carter first. Perhaps she would like to join us."

Miss Sully's poverty-stricken state was a knife to Millicent's already bruised heart. What had begun as a lark was now too painful to continue. Somehow, she had to find a way to undo the damage she'd done.

"Miss Carter has graciously declined," Miss Sully said when she arrived at Millicent's door a short time later. "I don't believe she has the constitution to withstand both mice and a bullfrog in such a short space of time."

Millicent mentally agreed. "Please, let us get to know one another better, Miss Sully."

"Ernestine. Call me Ernestine, my lady."

"Then you must call me Mary."

Ernestine smiled shyly at Millicent's request.

"You did well with Bryon's frog, Ernestine."

"I feel so badly for Miss Carter." Ernestine picked nervously at her threadbare skirts. "All of this turmoil is distressing to her. I am persuaded she's in dire need of this position. So much so, I have considered withdrawing my name from consideration."

If Millicent believed she couldn't feel even more miserable, she discovered how wrong she had been. If it would help the children and not destroy her mother's reputation, Millicent intended to withdrawal her name also. "Has Miss Carter confided in you?"

"No, yet I am certain of it. She told me she has lost her way through her journey in life."

Millicent swallowed and a sting at the back of her throat signaled her distress. "Oh my. That sounds ominous indeed."

"I only hope you don't view my speaking about this as gossip. I have worried for Miss Carter's sake and hoped you could advise me how to best help her. I want to step aside so she can freely have the position. However, in the end I fear she hasn't the constitution for the McDougal clan. I'm not certain I do either. In fact, I've come to regret my decision in coming to Scotland."

Millicent nodded her agreement. "If it is any consolation, I believe the children are acting out of self-preservation and not malice. It's their way of weeding out those who would not fit into their household to protect themselves from being hurt."

Ernestine smiled before she leaned back in a more relaxed manner. "Survival of the fittest?"

"You are a follower of Darwinian theory? And you have had occasion to visit the London Zoological Society. I believe you would make a fine governess for the McDougal children."

"May I be frank, Lady Mary?"

"I would prefer it."

Miss Sully's face drew into a serious frown. "Although I didn't say it, this place strikes fear into me. If I had even the smallest chance for employment in London, I would not have come *here*."

The very words Millicent wanted to hear came tumbling out of Ernestine's ingenuous mouth. Millicent's conscience felt much improved, albeit a temporary fix at best.

"What luck!" Millicent reached out to her. "Since you have trusted me, I shall do the same. I introduce what I am about to reveal to you with a dire caution first. I must solemnly pledge you to secrecy."

Ernestine's eyes widened while she gave Millicent her trembling hand.

"Wait." Millicent took a deep breath. "One more word of caution. If you are flattered I wish to make you my confidant, perhaps you should reconsider. What I wish to expose is very disagreeable. You will not esteem my friendship once I have revealed the truth to you."

Ernestine frowned and nodded soberly. "I have borne many burdens in my years, and I do not believe your secret could surpass what I have already endured."

Millicent's bad behavior cut deep as she searched Ernestine's face before she continued. "I have come here under false pretenses. I've lied. Should the truth come to light, my family name would be sullied."

Ernestine gasped and her pale lips formed a circle of surprise.

Sick at heart, Millicent didn't know if the woman's constitution could withstand the lie. "Do you want to stop speaking candidly? Am I asking too much of you?"

Ernestine leaned forward once again to embrace Millicent in a tender hug. "You honor me with your confidence. I will not let you down or allow you to endure this alone. You need someone, a confidant."

Millicent came undone. Normally not one given to tears, she began to weep. Ernestine held her tight to her bosom until her tears subsided. "I have come here pretending to be someone I am not."

Ernestine still hugged her despite her despicable revelation. "Oh, Mary, I thought perhaps that might be your story. You are not related to the Duke and Duchess of Weatherly, are you?"

"I'm more than just related. I'm their only daughter."

Ernestine inhaled again, louder, but didn't loosen her hold.

Millicent fought back the tears threatening to fall over the both of them for a second time. "If my mother finds out how I've lied, she will be humiliated. She recently published a book on manners when her own daughter is wickedly unmannered. If my latest foolishness should become public knowledge, my actions will hurt my mother's reputation."

"I have witnessed naught wrong with your manners other than your pretense and I'm convinced you had good reason for what you've done. Perhaps you could find a way to explain it all away?"

"Yes, that is what I'll do. I'll find a way to tell the children I've acted badly. For some reason it completely escaped me how I needed to set an example for them when I began this journey. In reality, because of my lie, I'm the least favorable choice as a governess by far."

Ernestine also appeared ready to weep. "Then we should find a way to make your falsehood go away, but a plan escapes me."

"I caused my problem, but you, my new friend, need to worry about your own opportunities. First, we must settle your future, Ernestine. If you had your choice, what would you do with your life?"

"I love animals." Ernestine blushed. "If I had been born a man, I would have devoted my life to the study of nature. But alas it isn't possible for a woman."

"How wonderful. I have a dear niece, Emily, who visits the zoological society at least once a week. Her mother, my aunt by marriage, is confounded by her intense interest, but still encourages her. Emily's only eight years of age but is just as determined as you of her desire to study nature."

"Your niece may have the financial means to make her calling come true," Ernestine said without the least hint of malice or jealousy.

"It's entirely possible the similarity in your nature to Emily's will serve you well in this case, Ernestine. My aunt is seeking to employ someone who will not try to interfere with Emily's enthusiasm. You see, although my aunt doesn't share Emily's unusual interest, she believes a woman must be true to her heart's aspirations. You see, my aunt is also a tad unusual also.

"There has not been a single female to apply for the post that has suited them both. The women applying say they have a devotion to the study of nature, but my niece's extraordinary enthusiasm soon wears thin for them. I believe your interest would equal Emily's, if I'm not mistaken."

"Your niece sounds like a wonderful child."

"Lady Jane, the poor girl's mother believes her daughter to be too timid. Even though she encourages her daughter's endeavors, they don't get along well in the end. They haven't found a governess whose personality is mild enough to relate to Emily, but strong enough to speak up to Lady Jane."

Ernestine picked at a wrinkle in her skirt. "Perhaps you could volunteer to lend a hand with your niece?"

"I have tried. I make my niece almost as nervous as my aunt does. Emily needs someone with both a quiet and mild spirit and I do not seem to master either quality for any length of time, even when I try."

"Why are you speaking to *me* about your niece?" Ernestine's voice sounded hopeful.

"Ernestine, I think you would be perfect for the position. Emily needs you."

Ernestine's brows furrowed above her bright and assessing blue eyes. "But why would your aunt hire someone she doesn't know?"

"My aunt would hire you on the spot with my letter of

recommendation. Lady Jane is a lost soul despite her displays of bravado. She was widowed even before Emily came into the world. My uncle was the love of her life and she has buried herself emotionally with him. She is only twenty and six, yet she is a social recluse."

"Truly, I would be able to take Emily to the zoological society once a week?"

"I imagine at least once a week or perhaps more. I shall spend the afternoon composing the perfect letter of recommendation. Trust me, you will love Emily and she will feel the same about you. Just wait until I tell her I have seen you petting a mouse and holding a frog. She will not believe her good fortune to have found you."

Tears started to pour from Ernestine's eyes and the sound of a heart-wrenching sob followed. "I will be forever in your debt."

"Nonsense, it is the least I could do. You've allowed me to share my dark secret without once chastising me for my foolish behavior."

Ernestine dabbed at her eyes. "But what of Miss Carter? Whatever can we do to help her? I wouldn't be able to find happiness if she is still unsettled."

Millicent agreed. "Together we will find a way to help. There must be a way. If we put our heads together, I'm certain we'll manage."

Chapter Four

With Ernestine's future settled, Millicent spent the rest of the afternoon with her pen and paper. When the gong sounded for dinner, it seemed more like a death knell than a call to sup. If dinner followed the example of the previous meals, Millicent couldn't be certain poor Miss Carter would survive to eat another.

Once everyone was seated Millicent turned to Ernestine. "I have already finished your letter of recommendation for Lady Jane. Also, you will find a letter of credit for your expenses to London."

"Is this Lady Jane so hard up to find help, she has sent you to the highlands to pilfer staff from us?"

Millicent was startled not just by the pointed words but also the deep voice—the voice of the highlander!

Her highlander.

She swiveled in place to glance at the doorway. She had little doubt she looked at Lord Maclaevane Mc-Dougal, Laird of the Realm.

Dressed in a McDougal plaid kilt, he was a sight to behold. He appeared ready for a parade, in full regalia. From his sword to his purse everything about him was larger than life. While not as tall as the red-haired giant Millicent now knew to be his younger brother, he was an imposing figure.

Millicent couldn't persuade her eyes to look away, or her mouth to respond to his question. She'd always believed she understood well the constitution of her heart. The organ had beaten steadily within the confines of her chest for nearly twenty years. However, suddenly it wanted to falter. Lord Maclaevane McDougal didn't seem to notice as he stared back, still waiting for her to speak.

"Papa, you are finally home." Caitlyn upset her chair in her haste to greet her father. Bryon rushed not far behind her. Both of them crawled into their father's arms as he bent to scoop them up. She'd heard the Scottish peerage took their parental responsibilities seriously and watched the exchange with interest.

Despite her unmannerly behavior, she visually digested him. The actions of the children as they enjoyed their father allowed her the freedom to do so. Any idea Millicent entertained about the man little Bryon would one day become, she now recognized as far from the mark. The artistic perfection of the grown up version left no doubt in her mind. His long, dark-reddish hair

glistened with a healthy sheen unlike the heavily powdered hair or wigs in London society. He'd pulled it
back together at the nape of his neck, where it fell to
the middle of his back.

For a man supposedly arriving from a journey, he
looked more like he'd been on the parade field. His
baldric crossed his massive chest to the large sword
hanging from his side. Two large brooches held the
thick baldric in place. One was encrusted with garnet
stones and the other with emeralds. Both matched the
colors of his McDougal clan tartan kilt. On the opposite
side from the gleaming hilt of the sword hung a shot
pouch. His sporran hung low from his waist and
reached down to his knees. It was made from the skin of
a red fox and ornamented with silver tassels and tags.

When he lowered both children to the floor, Caitlyn
began to help her father remove his sword. It soon became obvious she couldn't lift it. One of the servants
came to her rescue and took it from her hands. Bryon
took possession of the shot pouch and placed it on a
table by the doorway. Millicent understood how much
the children enjoyed caring for their father.

When Lord McDougal placed a kiss upon his daughter's cheek, Millicent took a closer look at his face. Not
even the slightest imperfection could be found in the
man's strong jaw. However, his eyes dominated his face
and entranced her. Beautiful eyes are nature's gift, but
his were an endowment of such magnitude, Millicent
couldn't comprehend. The harmony of thick dark eye-

lashes against their amber glow resulted in an arresting display of magnificence of an entirely masculine sort.

His smooth skin would be the envy of any woman at court if not for the healthy coloring from the sun. He wore no facial hair other than the darkening of whiskers wanting a shave.

As noses go, unless one had characteristics to set it apart, Millicent didn't concern herself with them. Still in all, even this man's nose needed to be addressed in her mind. Its straight Grecian form would make an artist's fingers itch.

When her eyes came to rest on his lips, she involuntarily shuddered. A proper lady would not dwell on those lips. Firm and full, they seemed locked into a permanent smile. When his smile grew, Millicent found herself like the proverbial snake in the charmer's basket, both transfixed and hypnotized.

As Millicent looked up to his eyes, she discovered the awful truth.

He directed his smile to *her*. She'd been caught! He'd seen her staring at his lips. Her face heated and she ducked her head to watch her hands twist deep wrinkles into her full skirt.

Another misstep in decorum.

"You have failed to address my question, Miss M."

"Lady Mary," Ernestine supplied before the housekeeper could speak.

Millicent lowered her eyes still further until her chin hit her chest and they had nowhere else to go.

Lord McDougal laughed much too loudly at her discomfort. "Lady Mary. You have survived your trek through muck and mire. I'm glad to see you have arrived safely."

"Yes, Lord McDougal. Thank you for your help with the broken carriage wheel. I apologize for failing to thank you sooner."

"And I apologize for not escorting you to my home, but I was on an important mission I couldn't delay. Now since you've avoided my question, I shall direct it to Miss Sully instead. Miss Sully, do you plan to leave our company?"

"I beg your pardon, Lord McDougal," Ernestine said with determination in her voice. "I intend to accept a position Lady Mary has offered to me."

"So now we only have two to choose from," he said with a sigh.

Despite her improved chances, a dejected look overtook Miss Carter's face. Her shoulders slumped and she suddenly appeared lifeless. Millicent feared tears were not far behind.

Millicent hurt inside for the woman's plight. Poor Miss Carter had certainly sealed her fate with her comment about smelly horses.

To give him credit, Lord McDougal recognized the woman's despair. He smiled at her and heaved another sigh.

"I'm a barbarian," Bryon interrupted as if sensing

the direction of Miss Carter's thoughts. He gave a dis-arming smile and a twinkle gleamed in his golden eyes.

"Our last governess said he's a barbarian," Caitlyn said. "And I'm worse. I'm a hoyden of the first water."

Millicent couldn't resist. "Well done, Miss Caitlyn. Unsurpassed perfection in anything is not to be taken lightly."

"I was beginning to wonder if you could speak with-out prompting, Lady Mary," her highlander said, mak-ing it impossible for her not to meet his eyes. "Perhaps I have underestimated you? Yes, I'm certain I have. And children, I will speak to you in private about your conduct during my absence."

Lord McDougal raised his glass to his lips, and then hesitated. "Miss Sully, since you are leaving us soon and have taken yourself from the running thanks to Lady Mary, would you still like to share something per-sonal about yourself? It seems a shame you've traveled so far and we know nothing about how you came to us."

Millicent gulped as she ascertained the direction the conversation would eventually take. The last thing she wanted to do was share more outrageous lies, espe-cially not with her highlander now turned lord of the manor. And not now, since Ernestine knew the horrid truth about her.

Ernestine looked at Millicent and smiled with confi-dence. "I am Miss Ernestine Sully and I have not previ-ously held a position of governess. Until the recent death of my mother, we shared a modest allowance, but upon her death the majority of the monies have gone back to my brother with the entailed family estate. I hope you do not think too harshly of me for my decision to leave. I am certain I would be more suited to a position as companion to Lady Jane Wainright's daughter."

"In London? You have secured a position in London?" Miss Carter said with a groan.

"Lady Mary has offered me a letter. She assures me it will secure the station."

Miss Carter looked at Millicent and a tear ran down her cheek. She swiped it away so quickly Millicent questioned its existence.

"Miss Sully, you were indeed a contender since you didn't shy away from Bryon's bullfrog or my brother, Lord Fen's, baby mice."

Both children moaned.

His Lordship looked first at one, and then the other. "Yes, Mrs. McDuffy has told me of your exploits. I will make it a priority to see you understand my displeasure with your conduct. Have you made your apologies?"

Both children offered a vocal apology in unison and then asked to be excused.

"You may be excused. However, this matter will be discussed later in private and at length. Be assured I will not forget about it."

Despite his threat, both children paused to give him a hug as they left. Millicent wasn't accustomed to public displays of affection and found herself staring again.

With the children gone, Lord McDougal turned his attention to Miss Carter. "Miss?" Her face was sullen and withdrawn. She seemed a different woman from the one Millicent met only the day before.

"I am Miss Victoria Carter, recently from Brighton."

"Your last post was with the late Lord Fogmire and his wife. Would you care to tell us why you left their service? Brighton is a far cry from the highlands of Scotland."

Miss Carter squared her shoulders and sat up straighter. "Lord Fogmire died suddenly and Lady Fogmire refused to pen a recommendation for me. I have no doubt Lord Fogmire would have given me a letter, but his premature death prevented it."

Lord McDougal nodded. "A riding accident as I recall?"

Miss Carter gave a curt nod of assent and kept her head held high. There was little doubt she was uncomfortable speaking of her former employer.

Millicent searched her memory for what she knew of Lord and Lady Fogmire. Lord Fogmire kept an apartment in London for the assembly of the House of Lords, but Lady Fogmire stayed in Brighton year around.

"Lady Fogmire refused to give only *you* a letter? She singled you out for this humiliation?" Lord McDougal asked.

"After Lord Fogmire's death, Lady Fogmire dismissed every female member of the staff without letters," Miss Carter said. Her chin trembled with the admission but her eyes remained dry to Millicent's relief.

Still, Millicent couldn't stop a rude gasp escaping her lips. To not have been given a letter was beyond the pale.

"You poor dear, to be released from a secure position without a letter is worse than never having had a position at all," Miss Sully said.

Lord McDougal raised his wine glass and took a drink almost as if he wished to fortify himself for what lurked ahead. He lowered his glass to look pointedly at Miss Carter. "It is very unfortunate, but for years Lady Fogmire has been known for obsessive and unfounded jealousy where her husband was concerned. I'm sorry to repeat such gossip in public but I count myself responsible for allowing you to state your case to us, publicly. My pardon for that. Had you sought another position, even in Brighton, I believe you would not be turned away."

Miss Carter lips formed into a silent exclamation of surprise. "You know of Lady Fogmire's jealousy, even in this remote place?"

Lord McDougal took another drink before he answered. "It is common knowledge and has been known for enough years the news traveled even as far as the highlands. Let's say no more of it. Someone should speak to Lady Fogmire." Lord McDougal's tone communicated his displeasure. "I cannot believe she has stopped to think of what an emotional and thoughtless action on her part could do to her late husband's good name."

Miss Carter sat a little straighter on hearing his words. "Lord Fogmire was an honorable man. In all the time I spent in his employ, I never heard even a whisper of gossip associated with his name in the household. Even if I were not the worse off for Lady Fogmire's actions, I would like to see the way she chose to handle his affairs upon his death, set aright."

"Good help is hard to find, Lady Fogmire should take care or she'll be mending her own knickers," Millicent said, and wished she hadn't as everyone turned to stare at her. She felt compelled to explain. "I know within the Duchess of Weatherly's household there are always more positions than there are skilled people to fill them. And, I apologize for my reference to the woman's unmentionables."

Lord McDougal raised a dark auburn brow at her spontaneous comment without a hint of what he thought. Millicent found herself impressed by Lord McDougal's heroics again. He behaved honorably toward Miss Carter.

"I would not care to return to Brighton," Miss Carter said, and thankfully caused him to look away from Millicent. "Even if Lady Fogmire gives us letters as you say Lord McDougal, I doubt it will put an end to all the wagging tongues. I have fought a hard fight as a single woman to keep myself above reproach. With one malevolent act, Lady Fogmire has managed to undo all my years of good work."

The hopelessness in Miss Carter's voice cut deep into Millicent's heart. Miss Sully sobbed aloud and Millicent grabbed her handkerchief just in case. If there was only a way to help Miss Carter.

Lord McDougal put his hand up as if to stop any further talk about ruined reputations. "I assure you Miss Carter, this *can* and *will* be made right. A year from now this ordeal will be no more than an annoying memory."

Miss Carter's eyes filled with tears. "I shall trust you are right."

With two women in tears, Lord McDougal appeared ready to dash from the room. When he turned to Millicent, he paused before he spoke as if he feared what might transpire next. "Are you ready to tell us what brought you to the highlands, my lady? With the wit you have already displayed, I find I can wait no longer."

Chapter Five

"I am Lady Mary Wainright, recently of London." Millicent understood he wanted to hear more, but she decided not to be forthcoming.

When the children came back into the room and all attention turned to *them,* Millicent breathed a sigh of relief. She would've been grateful for the reprieve if not for the look His Lordship gave her upon overhearing her sigh.

Lord McDougal stared at Caitlyn and Bryon as though daring them to speak first. "What brings you two back so soon?"

"Nurse is cranky," Bryon said.

"And we are very hungry," Caitlyn added.

"I see. And you've concluded I would be less cranky than Nurse? Very risky choice." Their father crossed his arms and leaned back in his chair. "Once upstairs you discovered your food would not be set before you in an instant. I picture Bryon complaining of his empty belly to Nurse. And she, sensible woman she is, told you it served you right to wait after your unmannerly episodes both today and last evening. Am I correct?"

Anyone seeing the children's startled faces could tell he'd guessed precisely what took place in the nursery. He impressed Millicent.

"I will exercise my fatherly prerogative to allow you to rejoin us. Nurse will wonder if I have had leave of my senses. Take your seats again. And take care to remember your manners."

He turned back to Millicent and she prayed he couldn't read her half as well or her ruse would be finished then and there. For the sake of the children, Millicent hoped not. Her bad example wouldn't be good for them.

"I was surprised to hear of you, Lady Mary," Lord McDougal continued. "Why would a lady of title travel to such a remote land and leave the social whirl of London behind at this time of year?"

Millicent wondered if she might be about to walk through fire. "My father was the second son of the Duke of Weatherly and died very young, when I was only three."

She could hardly get the words out. She stared down at her plate as she spoke so no one would be able to see she lied. A lump formed in the back of her throat and she wished for a great gaping hole she could dive into.

"I do not presume to know all of the English court, but I am certain of one thing"—Lord McDougal's skeptical tone only further served to shame her—"the duke has five sons and a daughter, not eight."

"Not *that* duke," Millicent answered. "I speak of the previous one, my grandfather. You are correct about the present duke. He has five sons as old if not older than you and a single daughter almost my exact age."

Millicent heard Miss Sully's muffled cough into her napkin, but didn't look up.

"I see," Lord McDougal continued. "So the grand-daughter, of the long deceased Duke of Weatherly has come to the highlands to become a governess to the children of a very *old* Scottish lord."

"But Papa, did you not tell us many times your papa's papa could have been the king of all Scotland?" little Bryon demanded.

"Aye, my son. But those days are long gone and we shall never see the like. We must content ourselves with what is and not what could have been."

He looked back to Millicent who neglected to lower her head before he caught her eye. "What makes you think you could be content to live a solitary life here in the highlands of Scotland, where there are no fancy parties or grand balls to keep you occupied? As the grand-daughter of a duke, you would have an opportunity to marry well, regardless of your purse, or lack of it."

This was a question she could answer truthfully. "True enough." She paused to sip from her glass. "It is precisely because of the social whirl I wanted to leave London. I care nothing for fancy parties and grand balls. Even the smallest dinner parties make me nervous. Do you have any idea how many times a day I'm required to change my clothes, or how careful I must be of each word as it leaves my mouth? It is truly exhausting to live like that day in and out."

His Lordship considered her words with a stroke to his strong chin. "What would you call a small dinner party, Lady Mary?"

Millicent thought of the dinner party to announce her mother's book the night she'd decided to quit London. There were twenty-eight guests. That was about as small as they got at Weatherly Manor. "I think twenty-eight or thirty. Yes, that sounds about the right number."

The look of surprise on his face told him she'd answered wrong again. Millicent turned to Miss Sully, who shot her a frown accompanied by a negative shake of her head.

"Is that too many?" Millicent didn't know how to repair the damage. She wasn't certain what she said that caught everyone's attention. Miss Sully's head bobbed up and down. Drat! Once she'd set upon a course of untruthfulness, Millicent never imagined it would be this difficult.

When in doubt, resort to truth, she told herself. "I felt compelled to leave London because I couldn't measure up. The Duchess of Weatherly has penned a tome on manners and decorum. You may have heard of it. *Gen-*

tle Manners for Modern Polite Society. I didn't want to be the miserable relation who failed to live up to the precepts it contained. I feared the duchess would become a laughingstock because of her close association with me. I couldn't live with the consequences."

Millicent could feel tears threaten. She lowered her head and prayed she wouldn't cry in front of everyone. Not because she was above crying in public, but she knew her tears would be misinterpreted. She didn't want anyone to feel sorry for her. She deserved the heaping hot coals of remorse placed on her head by her troubled conscience. One kind word would be her undoing.

"Are you a barbarian too?" Bryon asked softly. His voice told her he understood all too well.

Millicent raised her head to look at Bryon and forced herself to smile. "Not a barbarian, just misfortunate soul. On the evening the duchess announced the publication of her book, I elbowed one of her dinner guests in the ribs. He spilled his wine and the night was ruined. I thought it best to leave London under the circumstances."

Miss Sully's eyes widened. "You elbowed him on purpose?" As soon as she spoke, Millicent could see she wished she had not.

Why not tell the story? "The Duchess of Weatherly gave a dinner party to some of her closest friends and family to celebrate the release of her book and I had the privilege to attend. I sat across from Sir Henry Jarvis when he raised the beautiful leather-bound book high above his head. I had no idea the duchess had written it. It came as a surprise to me.

"If only I had not been about to take a drink at the very moment Sir Henry held the book in front of me. My wine went awry and traveled from the back of my throat and into my nose. The coughing, spitting, sneezing, and general commotion was bad enough on its own merit, but then Lord Finch decided to tweak me."

Lord McDougal coughed. "And you elbowed him in the ribs?"

"Not on purpose. Since he sat next to me, I didn't realize he'd moved his chair onto my skirts. When I tried to turn away, I found myself trapped by him. In my attempt to gain freedom I *accidentally* elbowed him."

"It's unlikely he realized he'd trapped your skirts. Is that what you mean about tweaking you?"

Maybe she shouldn't have started the story. "The very thing the duchess stringently stresses within her household went amiss because of me. Decorum. Sacred decorum. You see when I sneezed, some of the wine found its way onto Lord Finch's exceedingly white sleeve. He asked the duchess if she had anything in her book to cover ill-manners of the magnitude I'd shown. I knew then and there I needed to leave."

Once again Lord McDougal's golden eyes burned into her as he watched her too closely. "Aye, when you have a close relative who sets a high standard it makes it difficult for the mere mortals who walk in their footsteps. But in truth, Lord Finch showed poor manners by drawing attention to you. A gentleman should take care with the tender sensibilities of the weaker sex."

Millicent couldn't be certain but it seemed as if Lord McDougal did some tweaking of his own. "I cared naught what Lord Finch thought of my behavior, however, my . . . the duchess deserves to have the respect she has worked hard to attain."

Lord McDougal smiled. "Tell us. What qualities did you see in Miss Sully which made you offer her a position within your family? A position I am certain would have been available to you, if you had wanted it."

Another easy question, and Millicent gladly accepted the new direction the conversation took, hopefully one which wouldn't require any more fabrication. "Miss Sully has a sweet nature allowing her to sit quietly and not be obtrusive. But she also has a tremendously courageous spirit. I have an adventurous spirit only marred by an over-active imagination. I say this because coming to the highlands was just that—a marvelous adventure for me. I believe Miss Sully looked upon her journey with dread and probably a heart pounding in her chest from her foreboding. Is my assessment fairly correct Miss Sully?"

Miss Sully gasped. "Lady Mary, how did you know? There were times I believed I might even expire from the smothering dread of it."

Millicent smiled at her. "You have such a brave heart, Ernestine. I now know it was harder for you to come here to McDougal Castle than anything I have ever done. My dear niece would do well to have you as her companion. I know you will choose your battles well and do what needs be done on her behalf. I do not think you would back down when it matters in principle. You have shown that by coming here to the highlands."

Silent tears began to flow down Miss Sully's cheeks. Lord McDougal looked as if he might be ready to duck under the costly lace table linens.

"Well done," Miss Carter added, still dabbing her eyes from her earlier cry.

"I daresay, much the same could be said for you Miss Carter," Millicent said. "Although I have not come to know you as well as Miss Sully, I believe you have shown great dignity today. Far more than I. The very matter you did not wish to speak of, you straight out revealed to Lord McDougal and everyone assembled at his table. Without hesitation, I might add. This could not have been easy for you."

At Millicent's declaration, once again tears overtook Miss Carter.

Caitlyn appeared bewildered by the weepy women, while Bryon continued to stuff food into his mouth as if it were his last meal.

"I thought you would all think the worst of me," Miss Carter said with a sob. "You are so kind not to take Lady Fogmire's side."

"Not at all," Lord McDougal said. "This matter with Lady Fogmire will have a resolution to your satisfaction. You have my word on it."

Lord McDougal turned back to Millicent. "You've now given me reason to hire Miss Carter and you have taken care of Miss Sully. What do you say to recommend yourself?"

Millicent hesitated. Had she talked herself out of the position in a way which wouldn't embarrass her mother? She prayed so. "I truly wanted to see the highlands and wished to escape London. That is all and not nearly good enough reason to pass the post to me."

"See the highlands? And what do you think of what you've seen?" Lord McDougal's voice reflected the frown on his handsome face.

"Honestly, when I left London I didn't dream this place would have such appeal. All I knew of it was from books. From the moment I laid eyes on your highlands, I felt different. They took far more serious hold of my heart than I realized possible. It's like being touched by something more powerful than I'd known existed on earth.

"It's not just the beauty, but a feeling the place is untouchable, beyond human comprehension. The desolate mountains, glens and forests seem to say they will remain long after we mere mortals are gone.

"Of course, my first glimpse at this castle made me nearly change my mind. Once inside, I have found the additions comfortable, despite their bizarre design."

His Lordship laughed at that. "Aye, the highlands grow quickly on some, while others do not fare well here from the moment they set foot upon our rocky soil."

Millicent watched Miss Carter lower her lashes to hide her teary eyes. Could she be one who didn't care for the highlands? Millicent hoped not.

Lord McDougal stopped speaking to stare into space, much as if he peered out a spacious window to enjoy the view. "Then there are those of us whose life's blood stems from these hills. They are a part of us as surely as we are a part of them. There'd be no separating us from them."

The strong emotion in his voice stirred Millicent. Unable to understand why, it worried her. She tended to her plate while the serving staff generously filled it with the next course.

"So you have no personal recommendations other than your desire to see the highlands and escape London? I'm sure there are many who wish to escape London who would not take such a drastic step."

When Lord McDougal continued the conversation he surprised her. She'd believed the situation settled. Perhaps he needed more to convince him she would not be right for the position. "I have had a good education, but no experience with children. None at all. Even though I come from a large family, there are few children and no babies at all since my niece Emily was born six years ago."

Millicent thought of her five older brothers. All of them, although much older, still remained unmarried despite her parents' constant badgering for them to settle down and produce babies. Not a single one of them had fashioned a serious attachment, or any prospects of forming one in the near future.

"Lady Mary knows how to ride," Caitlyn added to the conversation.

Miss Carter appeared to be disheartened by the child's statement. Millicent cringed and once again felt compelled to come to Miss Carter's rescue. "I imagine all three of us have gifts to offer your children, probably none more outstanding than another, just different. And while Caitlyn may be of mind to reject Miss Carter, I believe it could be a mistake to do so."

Both women smiled at her comment on their behalf. Millicent didn't deserve their kind-heartedness.

"That is very gracious of you," Miss Carter said. "I fear I have not been nearly as courteous to you."

Millicent gave a dismissive wave. "Nonsense, you have done excellently. I'm not being kind. I believe everyone has a gift. My status among the ton has little to do with caring for a child. In point of fact, I believe often polite society ranks the demands of the season above the demands of child-rearing. I speak of this as a general rule and not how I was raised by . . . how I was raised." Millicent almost said by her mother and father. Perhaps it was time to sit quietly and allow someone else to speak. A mistake could happen in an instant. She intended to reveal the truth but not in front of the children. Then again, maybe they could learn from her mistakes.

If only she had someone to advise her, someone like her mother.

Lord McDougal's golden eyes burned into her as if he might be searching for confirmation that she believed what she said. It unnerved her. She wasn't the sort to become easily unnerved with a look. What was different about this man?

"Ladies, I have work I must see to. We will speak again tomorrow when I will give my final decision."

Chapter Six

Lord McDougal walked toward the west end of the castle to find his absent brother. When he discovered Fen in his dressing room, huddled over an open chest drawer, he laughed out loud.

"Fen, you have all the servants believing we should cart you off to Bedlam. Maybe you should keep your door locked so the staff doesn't have reason to gossip?"

Fen turned, a wide grin across his guileless face. "Would you have me upset your own children, Maclaevane? If they had not brought these baby mice to me, I might have turned my head and allowed nature to have its way with them. Your children would not endure it. They have promised to shave me bald in the night if I don't save the wee baby mice."

Maclaevane laughed in spite of the ridiculous story. "You spoil my children."

Fen huffed. "'Tis only to make up for their lack of mothering. You lack the feminine touch and deny your children by refusing to take a wife."

"If only it were that easy," Maclaevane said. "Saving baby mice doesn't make up for years of doing without a mother's love. I see it more clearly every day. Nor do I refuse to take a wife, I'm looking earnestly." And just like thus, the image of Lady Mary's violet-blue eyes came to him. If pressed, he didn't know what to think of how they made him mentally stumble about when she pinned him with her violet stare.

Fen laid a woolen blanket over the drawer. "Let's pray you make up your mind quickly."

"Aye, if only it was a matter of making up my mind. It takes two and I know how my decisions could make my children miserable. Recall the last woman who said she would take the place of their mother? Remember how blinded I was by her beauty? So blind, I failed to see her heart?"

Fen stood and made the room shrink by comparison. "I remember how we almost lost the children when they ran away and hid in the mountains, rather than see you married to the countess. I will not forget that fateful day until I'm laid in my grave."

"So it is settled. They do not need a mother unless I

can be certain the woman I choose will love them almost as much as we do."

"And where do you plan to find this woman in the remote highlands? Each day they grow a little wilder and make it harder for any woman to overlook their behavior."

"What do you think of Lady Mary?" Maclaevane winced at his own question. Fen was certain to make too much of it.

"Lady Mary, now? She's a bonnie lass, beautiful and braw. She didn't run from the children's antics. Bryon told me she has an aardvark."

"An aardvark?" Maclaevane laughed. "Not likely. How did he come to hear of it?"

"Aah, you will have to worm it from him. He wouldn't tell me. What *is* an aardvark anyway?"

"It has a long nose, big claws, and lives in Africa. I doubt she has one. Although I vow she would not surprise me if she did. She is an uncommon sort for polite society."

Fen stared too long and rubbed his beefy hand over his square jaw. "Have you formed an attachment for Lady Mary already? You have only spent a single evening with her."

"It's likely too soon to have feelings of a romantic sort. Perhaps it is *you* who have formed an attachment? You seem to find reason to seek her company." Maclaevane didn't care for the idea. Not in the least. He might be inclined to an interest in her if she showed any indication she felt the same.

"She gives of her time to everyone," Fen said. "She is a friendly sort."

"I met her early yesterday morning while I traveled to Loch Droma. I found her coach stranded in the mud and her hired men wringing their hands. I admit she made a favorable impression. Before I realized what I'd done, I asked her to step out of the carriage and into the mud. The rain soaked her, while she stood to her ankles in the mire and she never said an unkind word, not a single one. How many women have we met of such ilk?"

"The wee ones like her. Bryon speaks freely, but Caitlyn is guarded. Still, I know I'm right about her feelings."

"Don't get excited, Fen. It is too soon to know if Lady Mary would fit in here. Let nature take its course."

Fen growled. "Then I will have to continue mothering mice, and rescuing the household from the children's practical jokes. Each month passing, they grow wilder. Can you imagine when it comes time to present Caitlyn to polite society? Heaven help them then."

"I'd rather face the worst possible trick the children could conjure than spend another minute in the dining room with three crying women."

Fen's eyes widened. "What did you do to them?"

"Me? It is our Lady Mary. She adopts people's problems like others breathe air. If I have to suffer another evening of tears flowing over the tops of my boots, I expect you to join me to brave the flood."

"Tears? Yours or theirs?"

"You make light of it, but I nearly did join them at one point. Lady Mary has a knack of getting to the heart of a matter to drag even a man's tears out hiding. I would never have lived it down."

"So it is to be Lady Mary then for the children, Maclaevane? This will be interesting."

Fen's question gave Maclaevane pause. For a second he imagined Fen had more than the position of governess in mind.

As she awakened in strange surroundings, Millicent hadn't counted on her mother's lifelong teachings to be causing such internal havoc. The earlier whisperings of her conscience had become angry shouts. Millicent remembered her mother saying, *"When your conscience shouts at you, count yourself fortunate, for repeated failures to listen to it will silence it forever. Once you deaden your conscience, you are in danger of losing self-respect."*

Millicent knew she had to do something and fast. Any more lies might finish her off!

She decided to find Lord McDougal and make a clean breast of it. She jumped up from her dressing table as an angry Aphrodite reminded her of a cat's morning needs.

"Do you promise to behave if I let you out on your

own this morning? And do not chase the family dog. If we are to extend our stay here you need to make friends."

Aphrodite licked the already pristine white hair on her extended rear leg and responded with a curt meow.

Millicent made her way down the back staircase and allowed Aphrodite to go out for a morning jaunt on her own merit. She took care to leave the kitchen door ajar should Aphrodite require a hasty return, and then went to search out Lord McDougal. Not seeing him anywhere, she momentarily forgot her quest when she discovered the library instead.

The room smelled of beeswax, oil of pine, and rich leather without a hint of dust or mold. The delightful smell and the sight of so many books in one place tarried Millicent from her quest.

She made her way along a wall, allowing her fingers to stroke the volumes. Even her parents' library didn't compare to this one.

"Does anything capture your interest, Lady Mary?"

The deep rumbling voice startled Millicent so acutely, she pulled several volumes loose and they thudded onto the thick carpet at her feet. She swiveled in place to see the high-topped leather chair behind a massive desk turn toward her. The sight of Lord McDougal when he rose from his chair did nothing to calm her even though she sought him only moments earlier.

In her mind, he would forever remain the highlander in the moonlight over Loch Droma. Her accursed imagination made certain Millicent found it difficult to be in his presence without suffering the queerest internal havoc.

"Ahem."

"I beg your pardon, Lord McDougal. I didn't see you sitting there. And please, don't continue to stand because I have interrupted you. I shall leave you in peace." She wanted to talk to him, but the moment she found him alone she wanted to cry off even more. She'd never been indecisive about anything. Now, from one minute to the next, she jumped the fence.

Lord McDougal gave her a half-bow but didn't return to his chair. As a gentleman, he would not sit while she stood. "No need to ask my pardon, or to take your leave. I wish you to feel free to explore my home upon your leisure."

Millicent gave a curtsy and began to make her way toward the door. "Thank you, I'll come back when the library is unoccupied. Perhaps we could speak later when you aren't busy?"

Lord McDougal reached down to put his pen in its cradle and gave her a friendly smile. "There. As you can see, I am finished. There is nothing you can do to distract me. Unless, you have another pressing reason for leaving my company?" He raised a brow to emphasize his words.

"No," she said too quickly. "I mean no, your Lordship. Your presence doesn't disturb me. Not at all." Millicent had managed another lie without even trying.

This time her conscience didn't bother her. In fact, she'd eat with mice and frogs everyday of her life before she'd admit how much he really *did* disturb her.

"You have a magnificent library. Oh, good heavens!" As testimony to how rattled he made her, she'd forgotten to pick up the books she'd caused to fall. She walked back to where they lay and bent to retrieve them. As she reached for one particularly fat volume, she examined it in feigned interest. Anything to avoid his inquisitive amber eyes.

"All the volumes are yours to read. That one is written in French. Those in Latin are along the back wall. Do you read either language?"

Millicent quoted the first line of the book she knew well. "I read both," she said, before she replaced it in its original position.

"For the female descendant of a second son, you have misstated your qualifications. You have received more than just an ordinary education. Why didn't you mention that fact when I asked for your personal recommendations? Didn't you think reading French and Latin would have a bearing on the position you seek? I wonder what else you have failed to reveal to us."

Millicent could feel her face tighten into a frown. She needed to tell him the truth. If Lord McDougal offered her the care of his children, how could she accept? Not only could her deception hurt her mother's sterling reputation, it could also be detrimental to the children if revealed. If? Of course it would come to light . . . eventually.

Millicent had a difficult choice to make. Necessity demanded she speak of her deception, immediately. "Does that information change your decision?"

"No, I doubt you would be happy here despite your claim of the highlands capturing your heart. This is a very lonely place. Eventually you would have a change of that too young and very changeable heart."

Millicent wanted to protest, but in reality Lord McDougal was giving her a way to extricate herself from her self-made ruse. "I believe perhaps you are right. Now hearing it said aloud, I am certain you are correct."

He frowned as if she'd disappointed him. "I must be right if you relent so easily."

"It's not that." Millicent wanted to slap herself. This wasn't the time to argue the point. "I don't know my own mind."

"If you don't know your own mind, then you are much too young and beautiful to be my children's governess. I think it is unwise, at the very least, to ask you to stay here with us." Lord McDougal picked up his pen and opened the top drawer of his desk.

Millicent managed to hide the gasp threatening to escape her lips as he dismissed her with his action. Beautiful? He'd called her *beautiful*. Her tough decision just became harder. What opinion of her would he entertain when he learned her dismal secret? She wanted him to have a good impression of her. Her impulsive decision to leave London under false pretenses now became a millstone around her neck.

"I feel you are right. I am too young, although I feel I've already aged a hundred years since I arrived at McDougal Castle. If only I could start over."

"You have managed to surprise me again. From the night I saw you in the pouring rain on the sodden road to McDougal Castle, I thought you were brave. Nary a complaint, even as you were soaked to the bone."

"I thought about complaining when you said I was too heavy for the carriage."

Lord McDougal gave a hearty laugh. "I said no such thing. Your coachmen had managed to sink the wheel deep into the quagmire. I didn't think I could mend it, even empty. You believed I made a personal remark about your weight?"

"I fear I have a plaguing imagination. I can imagine a duck is a horse with little trouble at all."

Lord McDougal gave another hearty laugh and shook his head. "Why do you say your experience here with us has aged you? Have my children done more than what has been revealed to me? Perhaps something to do with aardvarks?"

Millicent thought of her cream-covered toes and smiled. "It isn't that. I would hardly make a suitable example for your children, since I am still in the process of making childish and reprehensible mistakes."

"In the process? That sounds very cryptic, but everyone makes mistakes. It is how you choose to deal with your errors which shows true character. Now you have managed to convince me you *are* the person for the position." He rested his pen in the inkwell.

Millicent was horrified. "No! What have I done? You must choose Miss Carter."

"It's too late. You have taken Miss Sully from us with a more desirable offer and now Miss Carter has asked to withdraw her request. It's ungentlemanly for me to say so, but it's partially due to your intervention I find myself in these dire straits."

She wanted to hide. "But I hadn't thought—" She stopped when he raised an eyebrow. She could hardly admit she hadn't considered how guilty she would feel because she'd lied about her identity.

Or could she?

Millicent decided to confess and be done with it. "The truth is. . . ." She was a coward of the first water. The words wouldn't come out. Not with his golden eyes searching hers. Not when he stood and moved around his desk with concern on his handsome face. He would hate her. She hugged the book in her hand to her chest.

And there was another complication she'd only recently come to realize. Having a young, marriageable woman in his household without a proper chaperone was a disservice to Lord McDougal. Her father could demand he marry her to set any scandalmongers straight.

"I wanted to escape London and the opportunity you presented was my way out. I believe I have gone about it wrong. It seems I have gone bankrupt of common sense, before I even understood I had a deficit."

As an indication her discomfort worried him, Lord McDougal held his hand toward a chair near his desk. "Please sit down so we might speak frankly. I think you have something you wish to say to me and are holding back for whatever reason."

Millicent sat on the edge of the chair and waited for him to return to his seat. Instead, he pulled another chair close to hers, much too close. How could she be expected to think straight with him so near?

Once seated, Lord McDougal ran a hand through his dark red hair. "You worry me greatly. I would not care for my children to grow close to you, only to have their hearts broken when you leave us. Perhaps you have someone in London you may wish to return to?" His Lordship stared pointedly at her emerald ring. "Emeralds herald success in love. Has someone won your heart?"

"The story of this ring is most unremarkable. It was a gift from the Dowager Duchess of Weatherly, my grandmother, on my seventeenth birthday. She gave me the emerald because of my May birth."

Millicent squeezed her skirt into a wad of wrinkles. "I can see why that would concern a diligent father to find a governess only to lose her when she marries. While I have no prospects of marriage, who knows what the future holds?

"Perhaps if I entered into a friendship with your children, we could avoid such a circumstance. As friends, we could always have the knowledge that no matter where we may find ourselves in years to come, our relationship would remain intact. I believe their regard for me and my family would be preserved if I were only a friend instead of a governess."

Lord McDougal still frowned. "Lady Mary, I would prefer if you would feel free to confide in me. If not me, perhaps you could speak to my brother? Maybe Fen could advise you with the problem you seem reticent to share with me. Although you have managed to convince me you would do nothing to bring anguish to my children, I worry for your sake."

Millicent wondered why he suggested she speak to Lord Fen. As he'd made the suggestion, he seemed to search her face for a response. Had she disappointed him?

"Thank you, Lord McDougal. I give you my word of honor I will do nothing to distress Caitlyn or Bryon." She meant it. She chanced a longer look into the man's probing amber eyes, only to glance away when her heart leaped in her chest and her stomach took a curious turn.

"If I have learned one thing in my life, it is to never ask someone to reveal a tightly held counsel until he or she wishes to tell it. I will not ask what you have done which makes you speak of bankrupt common sense. I will, however, ask you to take care not to disappoint my children."

"I promise," Millicent said and stood to leave. He rose also and extended a hand to stop her.

"No, do not leave, my lady. Sit. We have not finished."

Millicent lowered herself to the edge of the chair while Lord McDougal did likewise. When he inched his chair closer she had to restrain herself from bolting. Her stomach suddenly became the repository for all manner of squiggly inhabitants. Even with a vivid imagination, she couldn't fathom what would happen next.

"You have had a hand in making this mess, now you will take responsibility for it. I refuse to allow you to leave until you secure a suitable governess for my bar-barians." Lord McDougal's tone was stern but his golden eyes twinkled.

A zing of elation thrilled Millicent. Lord McDougal had just given her reason to extend her stay. She had no idea the invitation would be so stimulating. Was it the highlands of Scotland or the Scottish highlander mak-ing her wish to stay longer?

"But that might take a long time," she said, finally.

"Are you refusing?"

"On the contrary. Please tell the children you find me suitable as their companion, but not as their governess. Make certain they know friends can err where gov-ernesses should not. I will find them the best governess in all of Scotland for you."

"They have already gone through every available governess in Scotland, my lady. Why else do you think I posted the request in London?"

"Oh, my. I shall be here a long time then." She held his gaze and this time refused to look away. She sensed another zing of exhilaration for her bravery. The sensation was unique and not at all unpleasant.

"And, Lady Mary?

"Yes, Lord McDougal?"

"I promise *you*. You have done nothing for which amends cannot be made. One last thing. I received news from a neighboring village. A family I know well has suffered from a fire which destroyed their home. Something must be done right away and I must not delay."

"Of course," Millicent agreed. Once again he played the gallant hero. She dreaded what she'd make of it later—alone with her dreams. A highlander and flames? Perhaps she should not slumber. "When will you leave?" Her voice cracked when she spoke.

"I will leave within the hour. I know not how long I will be absent. Please look after my children. Even though you can't be their governess, perhaps you could teach them a lesson or two about manners. I worry for Caitlyn. Mice on the table! It is beyond the pale."

"I can't imagine where she got the courage," Millicent said. "There *is* that."

Lord McDougal laughed again. "I fear she has much more courage she has yet to display. Take care, for Lord Fen will be traveling with me and you will be left to your own devices. I hate to think of you in torment."

The sound of a loud voice raised in a near roar interrupted their conversation. Lord McDougal jumped to his feet and ran from the room. Millicent tried to follow, but his long legs quickly outdistanced hers.

"Get that beast away from my babies!" Another roar came from the bedrooms on the second floor of the westernmost wing. Lord McDougal didn't hesitate as he rushed inside one of the rooms.

Millicent arrived to see Lord Fen pacing the floor and moaning like a madman. Lord McDougal laughed so hard he held his hand to his side as though pained by it.

"It's a cat!" Lord Fen yelled. "Get it out of my room!"

"Yes, I see it's definitely a cat and appears to be pure bred." Lord McDougal laughed harder. "I think you should be grateful it isn't an aardvark."

Millicent's heart dropped into the toes of her fawn and yellow satin shoes. "Aphrodite?" She pushed Lord McDougal aside to see a fluffy white ball of fur in the bottom of a dresser drawer.

"Has it eaten the babies? What will I tell the children?" Lord Fen cried.

"The babies? Do you mean the mice?" Millicent asked. She had never known Aphrodite to dine on mice but she feared it might have happened. She moved closer to the drawer, afraid of what she might find.

Aphrodite smiled up at her before she nudged a tiny gray ball of fur toward Millicent with her nose. "At least there is one she hasn't eaten." When Millicent revealed the good news Lord Fen yelped.

Lord McDougal started to laugh even harder and she'd had enough. "You are no help at all!" she snapped at him and pushed him away from the drawer.

She reached down to lift Aphrodite. "Look, Lord

Fen. They are all still there. She hasn't eaten them. I think Aphrodite believes she's their mother." Aphrodite fought against being taken away from her tiny charges.

Lord Fen quit howling but wouldn't come closer to see.

"He is afraid of cats." Lord McDougal took no mercy on his brother as he continued to laugh.

Millicent couldn't believe a man so large and strong could be afraid of her Aphrodite. "No. Is that true?"

At Fen's timid nod, she turned her face away before he saw her start to giggle. However, Lord McDougal caught her eye and made it near impossible. She turned away to tend to her cat. Once she sat Aphrodite on the floor she jumped back into the drawer and lay down next to the mice.

"This is priceless," Lord McDougal said.

"What should we do?" Millicent glanced over her shoulder at Fen who showed no sign his agitation had lessened. In point of fact, maybe he had grown worse since now he pulled at his hair with both hands.

"What *can* we do? It would seem the baby mice have a new mother."

A loud thump and percussion jarred the floor under Millicent's feet. She turned to look over her shoulder. "Lord Fen has fainted."

Chapter Seven

Millicent made her way to the nursery after she securely locked Aphrodite in her bedroom. Neither her cat nor the baby mice seemed happy about the separation, but Lord Fen could not tolerate her cat. He'd made her swear she'd go to her grave without revealing what she'd seen happen in his room.

Who knew a grown man could become so worked up over a little cat? Well, maybe not so little. At least when Lord Fen fainted, his brother stopped laughing.

Fen had avowed them both to secrecy on penalty of death, a blood oath no less. Since Millicent had made blood oaths with her brothers in the past, it didn't bother her. But she could've sworn when Lord McDougal pricked his thumb with a needle and the blood began to pour, he'd nearly fainted like his brother.

One thing was certain. She needed to go to great lengths not to allow Aphrodite to terrorize Fen again. Then again, the sight of Fen's huge body sprawled over the floor made her feel right at home. How many times had her brothers' pugilistic endeavors produced similar results? A giggle bubbled inside and she took a second to gain control before it blossomed.

Millicent slipped into the nursery without alerting the children, not because she'd planned to do so, rather once inside it seemed a good idea. If she could observe them together when they weren't intent on mischief, perhaps she could gain insight into their true natures.

The cheery room gave Millicent a good feeling. Games, toys and numerous books left little empty space in the large room. The books weren't milk and toast fiction in the form of picture books, but tomes of character and substance sure to enrich the children's lives.

At the moment, Caitlyn and Bryon sat across from one another at a small table playing a game of checkers. Millicent knew of the game, but had never played, although her mother said it had become fashionable and perhaps they should learn. In London, taverns were the most likely place to find it and it was oft forbidden in the homes of polite society.

"I wouldn't do that," Caitlyn told her brother as he held a hand over a wooden checker painted bright red. Millicent moved closer, surprised they still hadn't noticed her.

"Nor that." Caitlyn placed her hand over Bryon's as he moved to poise above another empty space.

The boy's face tightened and twisted to reflect his deep concentration. The third time he moved his hand, Caitlyn gave him a big smile.

Millicent's heart melted. How encouraging to see Caitlyn found it unnecessary to compete with her little brother. Obviously, her role as big sister was more important than winning a game of checkers. How clever of her.

"I have never played checkers," Millicent said and watched Caitlyn turn in surprise. "May I join you?"

"Bryon is just learning," Caitlyn said, sounding more than a little defensive.

"What fun to learn something new. You should play with me Bryon, since I do not know anything about the game, although I have long wanted to learn." Caitlyn's frown didn't ease at Millicent's words. These children were close confidants which made Millicent an unwanted interloper.

Caitlyn pushed the game away in a huff. "I do not want to play this silly game."

Millicent didn't flinch. "Watching you just now I finally understand words from my mother I had failed to discern. She said she wished I would have been the firstborn rather than the last. She said I would've had the power to make my brothers kinder and gentler and tone down their rough places. Instead they made me too much like them. My mother said while learning to speak my mind could serve me well, giving sharp answers would not."

"Papa says conversation is the truest and best pleasure in life. What do you think?" Caitlyn's eyes narrowed.

"I would much rather enjoy a lively conversation with good friends than anything else I can think of. I especially enjoy when the people I converse with are older than I. In that way, I oft learn something new and interesting."

"Would you tell us more of what your mother says?"

Millicent understood. Caitlyn wanted to understand the mother and daughter relationship she'd never had.

"My mother has much to say on numerous topics and all of her words are wise. It would take a long time to reveal even a portion of the valuable information she has entrusted to me. I'm willing to share what I have learned from her, but first I have something very serious to tell you both."

"Did Papa tell you we asked for you to be our new governess?" Caitlyn asked. "We didn't have a choice. I still do not need a governess or a nurse."

Caitlyn surprised Millicent. "No, he failed to mention you asked for me. I told your father I could not in good conscience accept the position, regardless. Instead, I asked if I might try to gain your friendship. Friendship is far preferable in my humble opinion than the relationship of a governess and her wards."

Caitlyn sniffed. "I have friends in the village."

Young Caitlyn had an answer for everything but so

did Millicent. "In the circles I move in London, I have many friends, but not here in the highlands. I would love to make new friendships while in Scotland."

Bryon smiled. "I will be your friend."

"Thank you, Bryon. That will be very helpful since your father asked me to stay to look after you while he is away. He also entrusted me with the responsibility of finding a suitable governess for the two of you. Perhaps you might aid me in my endeavors?"

"Why can't you be our governess?" Bryon asked.

"I have told your father I am not qualified. I have a very big problem which keeps me from becoming your governess. I've done something foolish and need to make it right."

"We can help you," Bryon interrupted.

Millicent reached out to sweep his soft, auburn hair off his eyes. Evidently, she'd made one conquest in the McDougal nursery. "Yes, I believe you can—as my good friend. You see"—Millicent settled into a small chair beside them—"when I came here, I didn't consider everything it means to be a governess. My own governess had once been my mother's. I could do no wrong in her eyes. But I've been told of governesses who do little but find fault. Perhaps you understand?"

Both children nodded.

"While my governess thought I was exempt from doing wrong, others in the household were not so kind to me. I felt as though I lived under a magnifying glass since my mother's reputation called for perfection in everything I did or said. She required an exceptional daughter. I certainly have never been that, then or now."

"We don't have a mother," Bryon said.

Millicent felt petty. She'd complained because certain of the estate servants treated her unfairly? At least she had a mother to go to with her problems. And no matter what, her mother never once grew angry. Never once had Millicent's questions gone unanswered. "I am very sorry, Bryon. It must be difficult for both of you to have lost your mother. I cannot even imagine nor should I ever complain. In fact, I've never found fault with my mother. She always insisted I was perfect in her eyes. However, I always worried I disappointed her and she simply wouldn't say so. Now I'm wondering if perhaps I may have overreacted."

"Did your mother yell at you? Sometimes Nurse yells." Bryon pushed back from the table and moved his chair nearer to Millicent.

"My mother never once raised her voice to me in anger. Not one single time. Not even when I accidentally locked her in the cellar overnight and caused great concern for my father. Or even when I spoiled all my beautiful dresses playing with my brothers—every single dress in my wardrobe and still she didn't chastise me. She always blamed my brothers for whatever trouble I caused, never me."

Millicent sat back and sighed. "I wish I could be like

my mother but I know I am not. I haven't the first idea how to go about it."

"It would be nice to have a governess who never raised her voice," Caitlyn mused.

"That wouldn't be me," Millicent admitted. "I have a terrible temper. I once yelled at the Prince Regent of Russia. My older brother Andrew said I could've started a war, but I suspect he wanted me to run amuck for his own entertainment. He enjoyed taking the focus off his own behavior by using me.

"Although I'm bookish at times, I can occasionally be quite the hoyden, even when *I* least expect it. Just today I pushed your father aside and snapped at him. Trust me. Your father wouldn't choose me for your governess if he knew the true reason and flow of my soul."

Caitlyn's golden eyes blinked and widened. "Are you a barbarian too?"

"Your governess should never have said such an unkind thing to you. No. I am not a barbarian, just an unfortunate soul who wanders onto a dangerous course without counting the true cost. Hopefully, I have learned my lesson once and for all this time."

"Our governess told everyone we are barbarians. Did she lie?" Bryon questioned.

"The words of your governess were thoughtless and completely untrue. I think perhaps she tried to build up her own stature by making sport of yours. It is a common ploy."

Caitlyn scuffed her chair nearer. "She said the children she taught before us were well-mannered and never caused her to complain."

"My mother says it is wise to avoid comparisons in all things, but especially with children. No two children are alike and comparing one to the other is not only ungracious, it shows a lack of fellow feeling. Small hearts can be deeply wounded."

"I like your mother," Caitlyn said.

"I'm learning to appreciate her more each passing moment even though I have always loved and respected her with all my heart. I am sure she would like you too, Caitlyn. And of course, you too, Bryon." Millicent wanted to say more, but she was too close to revealing the truth.

"We will be friends, and if I see either of you take a misstep I will give you my mother's advice to guide you in the right direction. I promise not to speak of your missteps until we are in private, but you shall have my mother's wisdom nonetheless. I especially promise not to embarrass you in front of guests who enter into the McDougal household or anyone outside of it. It is awful to have others judge you from a single mistake." Millicent smiled. "Or two."

Caitlyn rolled her soft amber eyes. "Our last governess corrected us continually and so does Nurse."

"Remember, I am not your governess. I would like to be considered a friend. But, if your action with the past governess is anything like what I've witnessed so far, you will surely make it difficult for all of us."

Caitlyn stomped her foot. "Then you *do* think we are too bad to be our governess."

A sharp twinge of guilt made Millicent pause. "You have done your best to make me believe you are undisciplined, but I am still here. As I have told you, I wish to be your friend. Friendship is not abandoned easily and certainly not because baby mice and a frog disrupted a meal."

Caitlyn didn't seem relieved. "But you will leave us. You will go back to London."

Millicent didn't want to speak of what stopped her from accepting the position. However, she also didn't want the children to feel abandoned. "Remember I said I have a big problem which keeps me from becoming your governess. I told your father I have made a serious offense more terrible than mice or frogs on the table. I didn't tell him what I have done but still he seems to trust me with your care. I hope I can talk about it soon, yet what I did does not affect only me. It reflects badly on my family name. So I've gotten off to a bad start here in the highlands."

"Did you tell a lie?"

Millicent gasped. "Who . . . ?"

Bryon gave Caitlyn his hand when she reached for it. He gave Millicent a knowing gaze. "Papa gets very, very mad if we tell a lie."

"You do not *really* like horses, do you?" Caitlyn demanded with her lips drawn into a pout.

A sound at the door saved Millicent from confessing. The housekeeper peeked around the door frame. "Lord McDougal requests the children come to see him off. And you too, Lady Mary."

Millicent followed the children into the main hall where they found Lord McDougal with both Miss Sully and Miss Carter.

"Lord McDougal is escorting me to the nearest town where I can find transportation. To think I will soon be back in London!"

The glow on Miss Sully's face made her beautiful. Why hadn't Millicent noticed before how attractive she was? Lord McDougal might even be unhappy to see her leave.

"I wish we would have more time to become better acquainted." In point of fact, Millicent had hoped for a moment alone with Ernestine.

Ernestine reached for Millicent's hand. "We will see each other again, I am certain. I hope you do not think less of me for leaving before you have found a resolution?"

Lord McDougal gave Millicent a stare with his heated amber eyes after Miss Sully's question caught his attention. However, he turned to Miss Carter. "Are you certain you do not want to accompany Miss Sully?"

"I have decided to give Lady Mary a helping hand

until you return. It is the least I can do for the kindness you have shown me."

"Papa. Lady Mary is going to tell us her mother's wisdom. It is better than having a governess."

Lord McDougal bent to gather his daughter in his arms. "A mother's wisdom is always better than a governess. Listen carefully and maybe you can share what you learn with your brother and me."

"I will, Papa." Caitlyn threw her small arms around his neck and hugged him tightly.

"Papa," Bryon called and tugged upon his sporran until Lord McDougal leaned to capture him with his free arm. Somehow he managed to balance a child on either arm. Millicent liked the display of affection he so freely gave his children.

"The children have not been at all what I first believed. Their behavior is much improved," Miss Carter said later in the day while they were rearranging the nursery and Caitlyn and Bryon napped.

Millicent stopped to give her a smile. "That is because we are no longer a threat to them. If either of us had the dreaded title of governess above our heads, I think we would not be speaking so calmly."

Miss Carter laughed. "It is different here, since we both have decided not to seek employment. I had no idea. Sometimes it was exhausting in Brighton with Lord and Lady Fogmire. There is none of the hustle and bustle here and especially none of the dramatics. I find myself enjoying the slower pace."

Millicent replaced a book upon the shelf. "Be careful, we may yet call you governess."

Miss Carter wrinkled her nose and made an affable smile. "I only need remember the mice and that is enough to send me fleeing into the dead of night."

Millicent chuckled.

"Poor babes." Miss Carter looked toward the closed door of their bedrooms.

Millicent understood. She didn't want to be overheard by them. "It must be difficult losing their mother at such a young age."

That evening without the distraction of Lord McDougal, Millicent had a clearer understanding of what she was up against with her charges. First thing, Bryon pushed his napkin aside and ignored it. Next he found a fly in his soup and went on a lengthy discourse about it until no one could look at their soup, let alone eat it.

While Caitlyn picked up her napkin and placed it on her lap, she failed to use it. She coughed without covering her mouth or even turning away. Several times she used her hand to shy away an offending crumb from the corner of her mouth. Both wielded their knives and forks in a haphazard manner.

Millicent realized she hadn't paid attention to how the master of the house conducted himself at the table. Did she dare use London's polite society as a measure to advise the children? It seemed unfair.

Miss Carter didn't seem to notice or else said nothing even three days later. Each succeeding day she only commented on how likeable the children could be when they wanted. "The children are very intelligent. It is a joy to do lessons with them."

Millicent agreed. "However, their etiquette leaves much to be desired."

"I thought to say something to them, but hoped it could come from you."

Millicent dreaded speaking to the children about their manners. "Please don't make me responsible for teaching them table etiquette. Until I know what is considered proper in the highlands, I have taken a vow to hold my tongue in check."

"You don't suppose they are imitating their father?" Miss Carter asked.

"No!" Millicent responded too quickly. "I think not," she said in a lower tone. "When he returns, I will ask him in private to advise us of the customs here."

"But Lord McDougal has returned," Miss Carter said. "He requested our presence at dinner this evening at a later hour when the children will be abed. The housekeeper said it would be just the two of us joining His Lordship and Lord Fen, but I'm afraid I must beg off. I have neglected my correspondence for far too long."

Millicent wanted to object. Yet, how could she, when Miss Carter had done so much to help with the children? She could at least tell Miss Carter how much she appreciated her. "I imagine it a worthy goal for most to secure a place in polite society, whether it is as a member of the ton or a valued servant. To my way of thinking, what really constitutes *polite society*? Does it come to a man because he can trace his family name in history to honored ancestors, or is it one who counts riches as the mark of polite society? I believe it is not money nor title which makes for good association. It is the heart of a person, which gives one value, more than all else. I appreciate your value, Miss Carter."

Miss Carter had tears in her eyes as Millicent left the room. It seemed Millicent had found her calling . . . bringing tears to those around her.

Millicent had too much time at her disposal as she prepared for dinner with the McDougal brothers. At the sound of the first gong, she had already tried three different dresses. By the fourth dress, she realized the severity of her problem. She'd been raised in a household where the evening meal was considered the highpoint of the day—the entertainment. Sometimes it could go on for hours. She tried not to fret over spending the evening almost alone with Lord McDougal.

The dress she finally decided upon was one her mother would have chosen. The rich russet color was a perfect match against the autumn leaves. Her mother was enthusiastic about colors which matched the seasons. The color went well with the deep brown of her hair and made her skin tones glow.

Over the past few days, the weather had been exceptional. The warmth of the autumn sun pulled Millicent away from the stone walls of the castle. As a result, she took more color than she normally would. Even her very dark hair seemed to be shot through with gold strands from the sun. If the weather continued to be so agreeable, she wouldn't be able to show her face in London. No one would believe she hadn't taken to employing common hair remedies or toilette recipes on her face.

She braided the length of it and pinned it to the nape of her neck, in a very proper if not severe style. The thought of sharing a meal, alone with two men, even with household staff standing over their shoulders, intimidated her.

Then she remembered how comfortable Lord Fen made her. She'd never had the responsibility of conversing for any length of time with anyone of the male persuasion other than her brothers or father. If Lord McDougal chose to talk about horses, she would feel right at home. Anything else, she couldn't or preferred not to imagine.

At the sound of the second gong, Millicent made her way to the dining room. Lord McDougal had just arrived. With the table set for three, she didn't have to wonder where she was expected to sit. Both settings were on either side of the head of the table.

"Miss Carter will not be joining us?" Lord McDougal asked as he looked at the settings.

For a moment, he appeared as uncomfortable as she. That helped her to relax. "No, she has letters to pen. She's been a godsend with the children's lessons. She may not have been a governess before, but she is as good with them as any you would hope to find."

Lord McDougal held the back of her chair. "I was surprised you'd managed to convince her to stay with us."

"I believe she is staying only until someone else can be found and it had nothing to do with me. She is indebted to you for the kindness you have shown to her awkward situation. She told me you have promised her a letter."

He nodded and took the seat next to her. "Miss Carter is an affable sort. The children are taking well to this arrangement. They had only good to report when I spoke with them. Too bad we didn't think of this ploy years ago."

"I am so pleased you appreciate our efforts," Millicent said.

"You please me."

Millicent met his golden eyes for the first time since she entered the room. The effect momentarily stopped the progression of her thoughts. Millicent bit her lip as she considered how magnificent he appeared. With his dark auburn hair, not powdered and hanging loose over his shoulders, he looked every bit the dangerous highlander. He wore the same deep green color he'd worn the first night she saw him. One lock fell forward onto his handsome face and he threaded his long tapered fingers through his hair when he brushed it back.

His movements and appearance unsettled her more

than she wanted to admit. The sprig of hawthorn attached to the brooch holding his baldric also worried her. The sentiment of hawthorn was hope. Did he *hope* for something?

"Have you settled into life at McDougal Castle? The gods of the highlands have seen fit to send you glorious weather to welcome you. I have never seen such warm days for this time of the year." Lord McDougal ran his fingers through his hair a second time before he rested his hand on his leg. The gesture appeared almost nervous in nature. What would make a man, a score and nine years, nervous in her company? Surely nothing. Certainly not *her*.

"If I do not manage to stay out of the sun, I will have everyone gossiping in London if I return. I have taken my leisure in the sun's warmth more often than not. Once winter comes full-blown to the highlands and forces us within the castle walls, I shall be sad."

"*If* you return to London?"

"I misspoke. I meant to say *when* I return. I can see no way to avoid it."

"You make me want to ask what happened in London to cause you to leave us."

Millicent stared down at her plate.

"You are young. You must miss the excitement of the city. What do you think? Shall we entertain while the weather still allows? We should give a dinner party for you to become acquainted with the local gentry. The children could help and it would delight them."

Millicent didn't know what to say. She had no desire to socialize under the circumstances. Her dishonesty weighed heavy her shoulders. The profound mental burden would make it impossible to relax and enjoy herself. To make matters worse, sooner or later, word of her disappearance from London would reach the highlands. Wouldn't it?

"Stanton," Lord McDougal called to a man by the door. "Could you begin to put the word out for a fortnight hence? Invite everyone from a half-day's ride and back. Send someone first thing in the morning. And feel free to alert the staff at your will."

Stanton dashed from the room as though he'd been shot from a cannon. Millicent stared in amazement. One moment Lord McDougal had asked her opinion and the next he'd made the decision without listening to her answer. His amber eyes sparkled. He was enjoying the thought of entertaining so much she quickly forgave his lack of thoughtfulness.

"It has been a long time, my lord," another of his men said when he arrived to replenish the extra napkins on the sideboard. "Stanton is shouting the news from the roof tops."

It had been a long time since Lord McDougal had entertained in his home? Millicent wondered why.

"Aye, it has been a long time. Make certain Stanton tells Mrs. McDuffy so she can make her plans. And take care to plug your ears. Her screams will sound across the pond."

Millicent began to fidget in her chair. "What will be my responsibilities exactly?"

"I would imagine you are too young to become hostess for us."

He'd insulted her. She may be young but her mother had instructed her well.

Millicent could feel her temper flare. Yet he sat at ease in front of her with a smile on his too-handsome face. "How many guests will there be?"

"That is hard to say. Many are still busy storing up for winter, and so will not be bothered. Of the villagers, I'd say nearly one hundred. Of the landed gentry, perhaps thirty, maybe less."

"Oh," was all she could manage. One hundred and thirty people did seem like a lot.

"Of course, the villagers will have their celebration at the foot of the hill and not here inside the castle aside from a greeting and a toast. Many do not feel comfortable rubbing elbows with polite society—even highland society. Fen will see to the villagers' comforts. We have tents to erect and a couple of fat steers to butcher. Mrs. McDuffy has long complained she doesn't have room for fresh stores, so she will empty her larder."

"It sounds enjoyable," she said when she really wanted to run and hide.

"So will you be my hostess, dear Mary?"

Millicent tossed her napkin across her plate. She'd like to think it just slipped from her fingers, but she doubted she'd fool anyone if she said as much. How dare he call her Mary? How dare he call her dear?

"The gauntlet?" Lord McDougal nodded toward the napkin. He'd noticed.

"You c-can't c-call me Mary or anything else." To make matters worse, she stuttered. "It's not proper for you to use my first name. My aunt, the Duchess of Weatherly, has been married to the duke for two-score-years and she still calls him, Your Grace."

"I mean you neither disrespect nor impertinence. My intentions are honorable. We're less rigid here in how we address one another. In southern Africa it's the custom to rub toes when greeting. Calling you Mary pales when compared to the rubbing of toes. Must we stand on ceremony?"

Rubbing toes? Millicent's insides became agitated at the thought. "A man of the world should not believe ceremony is silly. There is a reason we must adhere to it. There are rules concerning propriety of deportment."

"And the rule of propriety I have broken in this case would be what?"

Millicent huffed. "Perhaps my bankruptcy of common sense has worn off upon you?"

Lord McDougal chuckled. "Aha, I am in the presence of unquestioned wit. I best beware or I'll end up looking the fool."

Millicent would not be mollified by his words. "For a reason which eludes me, you are trifling with me. If you are not careful you would have me believe I am back in London. You must know a gentleman should not become overly familiar with a lady. There are formalities."

"Mary, I think you may be teetering on the brink of revealing your true mind to me. I will not be offended by anything you say."

"I pray you are not offended, Lord McDougal. To become offended is to place too high a value on oneself."

"I'll keep that in mind. Did you chastise me in order to delay speaking your mind?"

Millicent didn't know if she dared speak boldly. "You do not subscribe to a certain very infamous lord's ramblings made public in his letter wherein he advises a woman should conceal her intelligence and not concern her weak mind with talk of politics, metaphysics, or the great mysteries of the world?" Millicent tried not to be overly concerned with the dictates of society, but she was in the end . . . her mother's daughter. She couldn't ignore what people deemed as the rules for polite society.

"Ah, Lord C," he whispered. "No, nor do I believe if women stray from domestic positions they will reveal themselves inept."

Lord McDougal had quoted from the public letters of a very famous member of the peerage. She tried not to gape, even going so far as to place her fingertips upon her chin to push it back up, should it fall and allow her mouth to hang open again.

Did she dare push the matter? "Do you believe, as he

further states, a beautiful woman should be content with men seeking her company because of her appearance. She should not want to be seen for the capabilities of her mind?"

"In my humble opinion, that is one of the most worthless pieces of trifle he has written. I have known many beautiful women who care for naught but themselves. I much prefer a woman with spirit and intelligence over beauty only. Although I have little desire to speak of metaphysics I must admit."

"Nor I," Millicent said. "However, I believe I could find much to say on many other subjects deemed for gentlemen's ears only."

"Interesting." Lord McDougal gave what Millicent concluded could be a nod of approval. "And have you had the opportunity to share your views with the opposite sex in London?"

Millicent wanted to say her brothers encouraged her to speak her mind freely. However, she could not speak of her brothers without revealing herself as a pretender. Without the energy to lie again, she revealed the only truth which came to mind. "I have never talked confidentially to any man other than a family member."

When he started to reach his hand toward her, Millicent couldn't imagine what he intended, but he stopped short of her hand resting on the table. When he stretched his finger and only a hair's breadth separated their touch, the intrusiveness made Millicent uneasy in a manner she'd never experienced.

Lord McDougal pulled away. "I shall cease my trifle, as you so aptly put. I do, however, find nothing amiss in addressing an equal by any nickname which suits. I call my brother Fen, and he calls me Maclaevane. It is a very amiable arrangement."

"And if you call me Mary, it is tantamount to saying I'm your equal?" Millicent wondered if he would take offense to her pointed question.

"That is exactly what I'm saying."

What could Millicent say to that? She could hardly take offense of any man who would call a woman his equal. Perhaps she *was* too inflexible. "Lord Maclaevane, please continue with your plans for a party. I would like to offer my help."

He laughed heartily at her compromise. "I concede and thank you, Lady Mary. Now back to your original question before I give in to the urge to trifle with you again and forget what you asked of me. If you would agree to be my hostess, I would be grateful. At your age, I already had a babe in arms and the burden of providing for all of the McDougal clan. I would never judge anyone's abilities based on age alone."

"Perhaps we could use the occasion to enlighten Caitlyn to what may be expected of her as she grows into her role as Lady McDougal." Caitlyn was already much older than Millicent when the duchess began to enlighten her.

"You take responsibility for the castle guests, so Fen and I can look after the remainder from the village."

"I agree." Once the words came out she had second thoughts. The motivations of this man were foreign to her. Her brothers had educated her to have a basic understanding of men, but this one with his fiery good looks eluded her. He didn't take himself seriously or place undue esteem on his own words. She wondered of his position within his clan, and of Bryon's claim they were descended from kings. Lord Maclaevane didn't have the haughty demeanor of wealth and privilege. Even Millicent's brothers, who all claimed to shun the materialistic pursuits of past generations, could not hide their highborn bearing, try as they might.

"We have not had a suitable hostess in residence since my wife died."

Millicent held her breath for fear he'd stop speaking and not reveal more. As much as she hated to admit it, she wanted to know about his deceased wife and she dared not ask.

"Lila died giving birth to Bryon. And even before Bryon, she did not have the constitution to allow her to feel at ease in polite society. She came to the highlands to escape the busy social requirements of her father, Lord Britley."

"Your wife was English? I had not . . . considered. Didn't Lord Britley retire in the north of England?" Millicent's heart began to beat faster. It seemed inappropriate to wish to speak of the woman he loved.

"Aye, Lila's father is now settled in northern England. Yet, when my wife was introduced into society, he took it upon himself to throw the most lavish gatherings in all of London. Lila didn't care for the fuss. I think she viewed the highlands as a quiet place where she might escape."

Once again her heartbeat became erratic just as it had from the first moment she met him. It was a strange experience for which she had no frame of reference. It happened when she spoke to him, looked at him, or even thought about him.

"You say you thought she viewed the highlands as a quiet place. You didn't know?" Millicent asked and then wanted to take it back.

"There is that wit again. Yes, after my progressive speech, I admit it. I never knew what Lila thought. I would ask, but she never felt free to reveal herself to me. My youth and inexperience made me foolish. I was only eighteen and Lila was seventeen when we married. I never pushed her to speak to me of what mattered to her."

Millicent hoped her emotions didn't show on her face, for his conversation stimulated her mind. She'd finally met a man with a similar nature and honesty to her own dear brothers. She could tell by his face he hated to admit his inadequacy to her. But, nevertheless, he did so.

"I often worry," she admitted, "not so much my thoughts would be perceived as shallow or of little worth to anyone other than myself. But rather as avant-garde."

"Avant-garde? That would lead to spirited conversations. Do you shy away from persons whose thoughts disagree from your own, or do you find it a challenge to discuss conflicting opinions?"

Once again Millicent longed to speak of her brothers who delighted in disagreeing with one another and especially with Millicent. She couldn't speak about them without sharing her deception.

"I love to express my ideas and thoughts without worry I'm being weighed and measured for them."

"Wonderful, then I look forward to lively conversations in the future."

Chapter Eight

Fen walked into the dining room polished and shining in his dress clothes.

"Am I late?" He gave Maclaevane a congenial wink.

Maclaevane tried to hide his frustration with his brother's presence. He wasn't ready to give up the delightful conversation he'd been sharing privately with Lady Mary. "Nonsense Fen, you can see we haven't started. It has been so long since you've come to the dining room I thought you'd forgotten how to find it."

"Did you forget you demanded it? You said something about tears and a fear of drowning as I recall. Have I missed anything?" The twinkle in Fen's eyes as he spoke made Maclaevane vow to seek him out later in privacy.

Mary looked from one to the other as they spoke. Maclaevane found it difficult not to stare at her. From the moment he saw her face lighted by the carriage in the rain, she'd intrigued him. When he discovered her destination was McDougal Castle, he cursed the reason which kept him from following her to his home. It had been so long since anyone caught his attention without any affection or theatrics. With his recent close call in the matrimonial arena, he wondered if he was jinxed. To have come so close to asking for the hand of a woman who abhorred his children scared him witless.

"How are your baby mice faring, Lord Fen?" A smile tugged on Mary's beautiful mouth as she spoke. Then again, what part of her wasn't a gift from nature at its finest?

Fen huffed. "You need to keep a closer watch on your furry white beastie. I am not convinced of her intentions. She lurks at my door day and night."

Lady Mary fought to stifle a chuckle and looked down at the first course placed in front of her.

"Why do you call my brother by his shortened name, when you challenged my request you do so with *my* name, Lady Mary?" Maclaevane asked. He could see a closeness developing between them and wasn't certain he cared for it.

"I apologize. I misspoke. Fen is a different sort of first name. Have you shortened it?"

"Let me tell her," Maclaevane said.

"I will make you pay, Maclaevane. Lady Mary, I have promised to behead anyone who discovers and uses my given name. Now do you care to proceed?"

Lady Mary's lovely mouth formed into a circle before she uttered, "Oh. Maclaevane is not bad enough? Your given name is worse than His Lordship's? No wonder you use the name Fen."

Maclaevane choked at her declaration. The amiable chit. Her violet-blue eyes were wide with delight.

"I promise to do naught to discover your name. Especially if it is anything like your brother's."

"Why have you decided to join us, Fen?" Maclaevane ignored Lady Mary's trifling or rather *tried* to ignore how it played havoc with his heart.

"The castle is awash with rumors of a celebration, so I came to see if it's true."

"The word is out already? But Lord Maclaevane only mentioned it minutes ago."

Her use of his name gave Maclaevane reason to pause. He smiled at her as she gave him a sideward glance. Her bright eyes rendered him unfit for further congenial conversation. Suddenly, Maclaevane wanted more. He wanted her to feel as free with *him* as she obviously felt with his brother.

Fen reached for her hand and she gave it willingly. Fen made a formal bow over Mary's hand and released her. "News such as this travels fast. We have not given the villagers a reason for a celebration for years—

almost seven. I have come to see what has made my brother want to join the living again."

Maclaevane gave his brother a look of caution. He wasn't ready to declare his growing feelings for Lady Mary. Especially since he hadn't spoken to her about them. However, it would seem they were seeping out for everyone to see. "I admit I am in rare form as of late."

Fen huffed. "For no apparent reason?"

Lady Mary remained quiet.

"I have a request, Lady Mary." Fen evidently was in rare form, too, since he continued to speak when he normally didn't have a lot to say. "I have been in forced seclusion with my brother and have forgotten my manners."

"What have you done?"

Fen shook his head in denial. "No, I have done nothing I'm aware of. I meant I need coaching before I misstep in front of our coming guests."

"You forgot your manners? All of them?" Mary sounded appalled.

Fen gave her a sheepish grin. "While we dine, can you advise me?"

Maclaevane found the look of dismay on her face interesting. Her manners were impeccable. Why would she balk at sharing her knowledge with Fen?

"Please, no. I cannot." Mary's delicate brows pulled into a frown.

Fen drummed his fingertips upon the table as if trying to find the right words. Maclaevane couldn't wait to hear.

"Would you have me humiliate myself in front of the woman I love?"

"You're in love?" Maclaevane exclaimed and his temper heated without warning. They'd just spent three days in close company and he'd not discovered this information. A sinking feeling came into his bones. Could Fen mean Lady Mary? Was his own brother falling in love with the woman who had begun a claim to *his* heart?

"Someday," Fen said and winked.

"You won't like what I have to say to you," Lady Mary promised. She seemed downhearted by the prospect if evidenced by how she wrung her hands. Indeed, she almost appeared to be on the verge of tears.

Fen smiled, unaware of Lady Mary's distress. Maclaevane could not think of why sharing advice with Fen would be so distressing. Perhaps Lady Mary had developed an attachment to Fen and didn't want to gainsay him? Maclaevane didn't want to consider such an option.

"Why? Have I already digressed?" Fen asked.

She sighed. "Are you certain you want to do this?"

Fen grinned. "Most certain."

She sighed again. "Then yes, you have already digressed. You were not prompt this evening. You could have inconvenienced someone with your delay."

"Then I shall arrive early next time."

"That will not do, Lord Fen. It you come too soon to the table, you will appear to be rushing. Someone might think you are rude."

"I have not even begun and I'm already a disaster." Fen threw his hands into the air.

Maclaevane watched their playful banter and grew more morose with each passing second.

"You should not have a seat at the table until all the older ones in your company are seated. It goes without saying, any ladies present should be shown their appointed places before you take yours."

Maclaevane grimaced as Fen mopped his brow.

Lady Mary cast a sidelong look in Maclaevane's direction before turning her attention back to Fen. "Please, Lord Fen, do not touch your hand to your face. Do not spit, cough, sneeze or heaven forbid, blow your nose. You will be disgraced. If it is necessary to do any of these things, you must leave the table."

"A sneeze? Isn't that nigh impossible to predict?"

"I am not the person to ask about a sneeze," she sighed. "And after you sat down, you began to drum your fingers on the table. No drumming, or humming, whispering or anything else to produce noise.

"If you are eating fish and encounter a bone, use your napkin. It is rude to spit anything upon your plate or table. Be careful not to allow food to fall upon the tablecloths and cause their ruination. This can be tricky and some hostesses set great store by their costly linens.

"Once you have used a utensil, you must not allow it to fall back to the table. Use your plate in this instance."

"Wait. This is too much."

"Lord Fen, I have only just begun."

After two hours Maclaevane put an end to the torture of both his brother and himself. "I agree with Fen," he told Lady Mary. "I'd rather engage in a sword fight than eat in polite society if there are so many rules!"

"Since I have not found fault with your performance, Lord Maclaevane, I know you are not serious."

Maclaevane smiled for the first time since they began to speak of Fen's manners. It made him happy to believe she found no fault with him, but then again, he'd been afraid to move.

"Is all else in polite society as bad as eating?" Fen sounded hopeless.

The situation worried Maclaevane. He'd allowed his younger brother to fall into a state where he could be made a laughingstock. Maclaevane looked to Lady Mary and saw she wondered the same.

"Do not worry, Lord Fen. Stay close to me and I will make certain you do not fail."

"Either you overstate your ability or you are lying to bolster my confidence," Fen teased. Maclaevane wanted his brother to enjoy the upcoming dinner party. He liked that Lady Mary wanted to help, but Maclaevane wasn't so certain he wanted his handsome brother sticking too close to her.

After her declaration to help, she became quiet. Not

even Fen at his silliest could cheer her from the mood overtaking her. What changed so suddenly?

"Lady Mary, I wish I could help you with whatever continues to cause you to worry. It's written on your face," Maclaevane said.

"If only *my* peace of mind were at risk, I would speak. I made a promise when I quit London. Actually, it was more than a promise. I made a vow to secrecy. I don't know how to reveal what worries me without breaking my word."

Maclaevane could see tears glistening in her dark lashes.

More tears? Maclaevane searched for a way to calm her. "You are making the children happy," he said finally. "I hope you find a way to resolve what is plaguing you so you might take pleasure in your stay with us."

"No more than I do, Lord Maclaevane. Now, if you'll excuse me, I shall retire."

Maclaevane watched her leave with a heavy heart. Perhaps it was just wishful thinking on his part to believe she might become fond of his children, or his home—or him.

Millicent found Miss Carter in the hallway on her way from the nursery.

"Did I hear correctly?" Miss Carter asked. "Are we to host a party for the entire region?"

"I need to talk," Millicent said. "I fear I may have made a disaster of everything."

Miss Carter followed Millicent into her rooms.

"Before Miss Sully left for London I confided in her. I would like to feel free to speak to you too."

"Please do."

"I know you think what I have to confess will not be scandalous, but it is, very much so. I have come here on a pretense. I'm the daughter of the present Duke and Duchess of Weatherly. And I have come to the highlands without their consent or knowledge."

"And now you are trapped. If you speak the truth, your family will be disgraced by your comportment. If you continue to lie and are caught you will fare far worse." Miss Carter gasped and clasped her hand to her chest. "Have you considered the untenable position you have placed Lord McDougal in? He'll also bear the brunt of it."

"My mother would know what to do and I have thought of sending for her. To make matters worse I took an oath of secrecy not to reveal my whereabouts for at least six months."

"Who would demand such a dishonorable agreement?"

Millicent decided to speak the whole truth. "I could not manage on my own. I had help to quit London."

"And you promised you would not tell."

"Yes."

Miss Carter frowned. "Are you certain you haven't made a deal with the devil?"

Millicent wondered the same more oft than not but a

promise was a promise. Once sealed it couldn't be broken. At least now she had a confidant.

An hour later, after many tears and recriminations on Millicent's part, she called Miss Carter by her given name, Victoria. Even better, Victoria wished to help. Nevertheless, even with two heads, they were no closer to a solution than before.

Millicent slept little that night. She was happy to have shared her true identity with her new friend, but guilty beyond belief of the additional burden it placed upon Victoria.

After the morning meal with the children and Victoria, Mrs. McDuffy peeked inside the door to tell them a carriage with a guest was on the road leading to the castle.

Millicent had never heard of such nonsense. Surely it couldn't be a guest for their gathering when only the previous evening the plans were discussed. "So soon? Could someone have arrived already? We have only just started to deliver invitations."

"Aye milady, and I willna' be the one to welcome this guest," the housekeeper said curtly.

Before Millicent could ask her reason for ignoring a guest, untimely or not, Mrs. McDuffy ducked away.

Victoria stood. "Go. You agreed to help. It is time for the children and me to see to our lessons."

Millicent walked into the main hall at the same time a lady and her entourage charged unannounced through the front door.

The woman pointed at Millicent. "You there, watch

after the men responsible and make certain my trunks are not damaged."

Millicent hesitated. At first it didn't register she'd been mistaken for a servant by the woman. The tactless request may not have been intentionally unkind, so Millicent took a second to consider her own words before she responded in kind.

"What is wrong with you? Are you addled? Do not just stand there. See to my trunks this minute."

Millicent didn't want to take umbrage. She made a mental note to bring more lanterns into the dreary hall if it was so dark the woman couldn't see. "I'm sorry," Millicent said. "I—"

"And make certain someone brings me a tray of food. Perhaps bread and cheese. I know the way to my rooms. And wine. I need a glass of mulled wine right away. Take care the bread is fresh and the wine is aged. Do you think you can handle that?"

Millicent could feel her temper rising. Who was this woman to demand service in another's household? "Perhaps you would like a lesson in manners?"

"How dare you—"

"Have you not been taught the use of a knocker? Since you barge inside on your own initiative, please give the household time to respond properly."

The woman's face colored, but Millicent suspected anger brought the pink.

"Where is His Lordship's housekeeper? She is well

acquainted with my tastes. It is not as if *you* will be serving me."

Millicent nodded. "That is the first thing you have said correctly since you flew through the door."

"How dare you speak to me this way? Leave my presence immediately and do not return or I will have you—"

"Countess?" Lord McDougal's voice over Millicent's shoulder stopped her from saying something more. "I see you have met Lady Mary."

Millicent wondered what the woman had been about to threaten.

"*Lady* Mary?" the woman huffed. Millicent watched the name register on her beautiful face. "I thought this woman was a servant."

"Lady Mary, may I present the Countess Rachessa. Formerly of the highlands before she married a French count. Now she's returned to us a rich widow."

Millicent understood the cut Lord McDougal made with his silky tone. "Countess, I assume you are familiar with the Duke and Duchess of Weatherly?"

The countess gasped. "Are you related to the Duke and Duchess of Weatherly?"

Millicent didn't want to answer. "Yes," would have to suffice.

"In what way are you related?" The rude countess continued to be a nuisance.

One of the footmen still holding a heavy case took a step forward.

Millicent used his gesture to overlook the countess's question.

Lord McDougal took pity on the man. "I shall get Mrs. McDuffy to show you where to put the countess's luggage."

The countess's demeanor changed when she turned to Lord McDougal. "I know where my rooms are."

"All of our guests will be taken to the south wing," Lord McDougal said, and the countess jerked as though he'd slapped her. "Please, take her luggage there."

Millicent could see the woman wanted to argue. If not for the earlier disruption, she more than likely would have done so and perhaps even eagerly.

"Maclaevane, I hadn't realized you've renewed your London ties," the countess said with a pout. "What brings you to the highlands, Lady Mary?"

Maclaevane? The countess used his name in such a way which would leave little doubt in the hearer's minds as to their relationship. The countess was on intimate terms with Lord McDougal.

"His Lordship did not bring me from London. I came to seek a position as governess for the children."

"That explains it then," the countess said, and waved her hand to discharge Millicent.

Completely dismissed from the countess's attention, Millicent watched her move closer to Lord McDougal. "I need rest after my travel. Perhaps I will see you at tea?"

"I had planned on having tea in the nursery today with Lady Mary and Miss Carter," His Lordship said.

"Would you care to join us there with my children? I am certain they have much they would like to say to you."

The woman simpered and then proceeded to allow her lips to quiver. Her bosom heaved with a prolonged sigh before she rolled her head to one side and then batted her eyes. "Maclaevane, I was hoping to have you to myself. It has been so long since I have been asked to visit McDougal Castle."

Millicent had enough of the woman's conceited contortions. If this was the type of woman whose company Lord McDougal sought, Millicent needed to reassess her opinion of him. "If you will please excuse me." She gave the woman a curtsy. "I will send the housekeeper to your room with a tray of food and wine as you requested."

Millicent turned to leave before she said something she would later regret.

"You are mistaken," Millicent heard the countess say to her back and stopped. "Why would I require a plate of food?"

Millicent turned back to face the woman. "Did you not request a plate of bread and cheese? And a glass of mulled wine?"

"Why would I request wine so early in the day? It is still morning. You are mistaken."

If only the two of them were in the room, Millicent would have spoken freely. However, there were others to be considered. Even if Millicent had no respect for the countess, she did esteem Lord McDougal and did not want to inflict a grievance upon him. "My apologies. Perhaps one of your footmen made the request of me."

The countess sputtered as if trying to think of a reply. One of her men almost smiled.

"I will see to Countess Rachessa," Lord Maclaevane said. Millicent turned away before he could see how disappointed he'd just made her.

"Please join us for tea, Countess Rachessa," Millicent said before she walked away. With each step she grew angrier. Hadn't Lord Maclaevane just spoken of beautiful women who cared for naught except their own creature comforts? Was he blind? Had the countess fooled him with finery fit for a painted peacock?

Millicent went to the library where she doubted the countess had once ever set foot. She intended to make a list of necessary tasks to accomplish before all the guests arrived. And she purposely forgot to request the countess's food and wine.

Sometime later, the sound of footsteps drew her attention from her task.

"What have I done to anger you?"

At the sound of Lord Maclaevane's deep voice, Millicent looked up from her pen and paper. "I'm sure I have no idea what you mean. Perhaps my hearing problem has caused another oversight?"

"What hearing . . . the countess? I understand why you would not be happy with the countess, but why are you piqued with me? What have I done to distress you?"

"I am a visitor in your home. I have no claim to opinions on how you choose to handle your affairs." Millicent winced at how her words came out. Why *was* she so angry with him? He'd done nothing. Absolutely nothing.

"Aha, for a moment I thought perhaps you might be jealous of the countess."

His assumption dismayed her.

Lord Maclaevane didn't wait on a reply. As he walked away, Millicent tried to think of a retort.

Something.

Anything?

By the time he'd closed the door behind him, she still had nothing in mind to suffice.

Jealous of the countess? How dare he.

Chapter Nine

When the countess failed to come to tea in the nursery, Millicent couldn't help but be relieved. Lord Maclaevane spent the time wisely in conversation with his children, but even his witty dialog didn't ease her temper. She knew it showed. Even if she found it difficult to control her bad humor, she had experience not allowing it to show. It took a great deal for her to resort to bickering. Neither a trifling, nor the bitterest divergence could make her lose control of her tongue at that moment.

Please?

Bryon wanted to talk about the dinner party and nothing else. Caitlyn seemed uncomfortable, but Lord Maclaevane appeared unaware of her discomfort. Millicent caught him looking at her on the sly. She wondered if he'd purposely challenged her to see her reaction.

Was she jealous? Could it be true? Had she formed an attachment to him so easily as to make her foolish and unhinged?

"Will the countess come to the party?" Caitlyn asked.

Millicent finally understood what bothered the young girl.

"Countess Rachessa has already arrived." Millicent watched a frown blossom on her youthful face. "Take care you are not accused of jealousy." Once uttered, the words would not return even though Millicent held her mouth wide to beckon their return. Hadn't she only seconds ago made a silent promise to not lose control?

Lord McDougal continued chewing taffy as though Millicent hadn't made a very tactless remark.

Why had she believed him to be heroic? The man was obtuse! She needed to leave before she made a vocal blunder he would not soon forget. "If you'll excuse me, I have to plan for a party and need peace and quiet."

Lord Maclaevane stood with her. "I have much to do also. Lady Mary, will I have the pleasure of your company at dinner? Miss Carter, will you please join us too this evening?"

"Please, Victoria," Millicent said. "Lord Fen will be happy to have another friendly face as he undergoes trial by fire."

Since His Lordship waited to walk with her, Millicent had no choice. "Good afternoon, Lord McDougal," she said tersely in the hopes he would continue on his way without her.

"Are we back to formalities then? I am no longer Lord Maclaevane to you?"

Millicent didn't want to have a personal conversation in the nursery in front of witnesses. "I think it's easier to teach by example. Do you want your children to know what is deemed proper in London and what is not?"

He turned to his children. "Listen to what Lady Mary tells you is proper in London. However, if you also wish to know what is acceptable here in the highlands, ask her. If she doesn't know, she can ask me."

He knew full well she would not argue the point in front of his children. His self-satisfied smile spoke volumes. Somehow she restrained the growl building in her throat and walked in the opposite direction. To give him credit, he didn't follow. How had everything gone awry so fast? What had happened to her gallant highlander?

Later, at the sound of the first dinner gong, Millicent was already dressed and ready. A knock on her door kept her from changing her mind about her choice of dresses. In London, she never gave a second thought to what she wore. Now, in the highlands, where it should matter even less, Millicent didn't seem to know her own mind. She opened her door to find Victoria, who wore the same frock from that morning.

"I have come to tell you I shall not come to dinner. If

I questioned if I was welcome before, I certainly do not feel so now. I am a servant." Victoria's mottled and blotched face betrayed she'd been crying.

Millicent had an idea of what or who Victoria had encountered to bring her to tears. "The countess? What did she do?"

Victoria huffed. "The countess, indeed. I could not eat a single morsel from the same table as *that* woman. When I think of the poor children, it makes me ill. And I had come to view His Lordship as an admirable man. Any man who falls for the countess is a fool."

Victoria placed her hand over her mouth. "I have said too much."

Falls for the countess? Millicent's chest hurt. She didn't want to believe the Countess Rachessa had won Lord McDougal's heart. "What happened?"

Victoria walked into the room and waited until Millicent secured the door behind them before she spoke. "The countess called me a liar to my face when I told her I was tutoring the children."

"She is outspoken and oft wrong. I understand why you do not wish to join us, but I will feel like a sheep going to the slaughter without you. Since the countess took an immediate dislike to me, I fear I will fare no better than you. Will you not reconsider? Please?"

Victoria began to pace. "I'm sorry, but I cannot. Something must be done. Her beauty must blind Lord McDougal. We can't allow the children to suffer because of it. It is up to you to see it doesn't happen."

Millicent grimaced. She didn't want to discuss Lord Maclaevane's feelings for the countess. She didn't want to believe it was possible. "His Lordship boasts to be above falling for a woman because of her beauty. Why do you think the children will suffer from his dealings with the countess?"

"Caitlyn says the countess is to become her father's wife and their mother. Caitlyn is hysterical. I told her I would talk to you and perhaps find a way to . . . I'm not sure what can be done. We must find a way to protect the children."

The backs of Millicent's eyelids burned and her throat hurt. She could feel tears beginning and walked to the window with her back to Victoria. "Lord McDougal and the countess are to be married?"

"That is what the countess has told Caitlyn. I don't believe there has been a formal announcement yet. And if there hasn't been, perhaps we can ruin the countess's plans."

Millicent touched the tips of her fingers to the windowpane and tried to breathe normally. "What if Lord McDougal truly cares for the countess? Certainly we should not interfere in that case. If he loves her, it is none of our concern and we must trust he will protect the children."

"Let's put him to the test," Victoria continued as if Millicent's heart had not been shattered. "If it is womanly beauty which draws him, you are far more striking than the countess. Let me help you get ready for dinner. I will do your hair. Show me your dresses."

"I am already dressed."

"That frock will not do. And why do you wear your hair so tight against your head? Perhaps you should wear it down."

Wear it down?

Shocking!

Millicent at first tried to argue with Victoria, but the woman turned into a demon once her mind became set. It was much easier to numb her mind while she listened to Victoria's chatter. Even at the sound of the second gong, Millicent was not ready.

Victoria chose a warm, wine-colored silk with molded sleeves under bouffant caps. The skirts were full and bustled in the back with a long train. The bodice, in the cuirass mode, made her appear to be clothed in a corset from the waist upward. Victoria promised the low neckline would be the perfect foil against the poor countess. Millicent couldn't understand what she meant and was afraid to ask.

Victoria worked Millicent's garnet-and-diamond-studded combs into the stylish upsweep. When she finished, Millicent could not believe her eyes. And her relief to not have her hair flying free almost made her giddy. "You are a miracle worker."

"Nonsense, you have given me more to work with than Lady Fogmire ever did."

When Millicent walked into the dining room a hush fell over the room, and she nearly bolted.

Lord Fen rushed to her side "Lady Mary? I have been lost without you."

He gave her his arm and leaned close. "You are beautiful this evening. Did you forget the rule on tardiness?" he whispered.

"No whispering. Will you show me to my seat?" As she walked with Fen, Lord Maclaevane shut his gaping mouth and offered his arm to the countess. His relationship with the countess must have hit a snag, for he resembled a thundercloud. "And you are right, Lord Fen. I am tardy and ask your forgiveness if I have inconvenienced anyone."

"Countess Rachessa only just arrived, so you are not the only one tardy."

Millicent cast a sidelong look to the countess, who examined Millicent's garments with narrowed eyes.

When Lord Maclaevane pulled out a chair for the countess to sit, the woman looked away from Millicent. She shook her head and refused. "No, this seat must be for your governess."

"I don't have a governess." He met Millicent's eyes for the briefest moment.

Lord Maclaevane left the countess to her own devices and went to stand at his customary place at the head of the table. Fen seated Millicent on His Lordship's right before taking the seat on the other side of her. A place had been set for the countess on the right of Fen, far from Lord Maclaevane, but she didn't sit. Both men stood behind their chairs and waited patiently for her.

After a time the countess walked around the table to take hold of the chair on the other side of Lord Maclaevane. "I should have this seat next to His Lordship."

"The seating is fine the way it is," Lord Maclaevane said testily. The countess ignored him and signaled to the nearest servant.

"Move my service here."

Millicent had already had enough of the countess's demands and the meal hadn't yet begun. She turned and leaned close to Lord Fen. "Lord Fen, shall we continue our lessons then?"

Lord Fen peered at the countess and frowned. Millicent understood he didn't want the woman to know his deficiencies. To his considerable credit, he nodded anyway.

"As a true sign of his commendable nature, Lord Fen has agreed to continue our discussion on comportment," Millicent announced. "Lord Fen, please take note of how the countess addressed His Lordship's staff. Because someone is in your employ does not give one leave to be discourteous. In fact, if we have superior advantages in life, we should take extra measures to be kind and considerate of those who see to our personal needs. Should I have felt it necessary to change the settings of Lord McDougal's table—although I assure you, I would not—I would first beg forgiveness for my demands, and then I would take care to use 'please' and 'thank you' with my request."

The countess started to protest but, Lord Maclaevane talked over her. "Lady Mary is giving Lord Fen lessons on manners. Isn't she clever? However, Lady Mary, correct me if I err. Is it not true a guest should not seek to sit at the upper end of the table unless at the master's request?"

Millicent started to relax and put her napkin to her mouth for a moment to hide her smile. "It is true. The master of the house will have it his way as is his due. It may trouble the others present at the table when matters do not proceed as planned."

Lord Maclaevane gave a nod of assent. "You look especially lovely this evening Lady Mary, more than lovely. I agree with Fen's earlier words, you are beautiful." He leaned in her direction and she pulled back. "You too, countess," he added, but didn't take his gaze from Millicent's face.

Perhaps Victoria had made the correct assumption. Millicent couldn't decide if it pleased her or not. She hated to believe he might be a shallow sort.

The countess pinned Lord Maclaevane with a heated gaze and her lips formed a pout. "What do you mean, you don't have a governess? Who is Mary then?" The shrill notes of her tone showed her petulance.

Millicent gave the countess an amiable smile and took care to remain graceful in both speech and manner. "See there, Lord Fen, how wonderful. The countess has just shown you another example to avoid by addressing me as a familiar. The name Lady Mary is a legal title I received upon my birth. Unless I give leave of someone to use my first name only, they should not. My aunt, the duchess, has never called her husband the duke by his first name."

The countess sputtered, but once again Lord Maclaevane spoke over her. "Brilliantly done, Countess! What do you think, Fen?"

Lord Fen smiled and nodded. "It is much easier this evening. I am even enjoying my lessons."

The countess feigned a simpering laugh as if she, too, enjoyed Lord Fen's lessons.

"You are very good at this, Countess," Millicent said. "Did you hear the countess laugh just then, Lord Fen? Please remember the sound in the future. If there is something worthy of enjoyment, show it with a hearty laugh. Do not simper. It is as rude to simper as it is to be overly loud and boisterous."

"I'll remember," Lord Fen promised and then looked pointedly at the countess as if he awaited further demonstration of what *not* to do.

Millicent noticed the countess appeared nervous as she glanced back and forth between Lord McDougal and Millicent. She picked up her knife and fork and held them upright on either side of her plate. Millicent supposed the countess did so to signal she wanted to be served.

"There again, the countess holds her silver upright.

Neither do it before the meal or during. It's common to forget in the midst of a rousing conversation, but you must restrain yourself, Lord Fen."

The countess dropped her silver across her plate as though it burned her hand. When she saw Millicent looking, she quickly picked it back up again. "What have I done now?

"You should not cross your knife and fork upon your plate until you have finished. It is a sign for those serving to remove your plate."

The countess narrowed her eyes. "I did not do it on purpose. I can hardly be finished when I've yet to begin. Besides, I am near ready to expire for hunger. My stomach is growling loud enough to be heard across the moors."

"Is that like drumming one's fingers on the table?" Lord Fen asked.

As the meal progressed, Millicent almost felt sorry for the countess. If not for the woman's acid tongue, Millicent would have ceased her ploy. What surprised her most was Lord Maclaevane. He seemed to be enjoying the evening and on more than one occasion pointed out the countess's inappropriate manners— under the guise of what Lord Fen should avoid, of course.

When her conscience finally took over, Millicent begged to retire. "If I had a meeker disposition I may have enjoyed London more and I don't ascribe to knowing all about manners. Since I cannot seem to keep my mouth shut at the times when it is most necessary, I am always left with a feeling of impending doom hanging over my head. The most inappropriate occurrences await me at every twist and turn. Try as I might, I cannot foresee them."

Lord Maclaevane laughed heartily at her statement. "Like finding poor quiet souls a place of employment when you yourself seek a position? Or pointing out the logical progression of a conversation when the speaker had not thought how their words would come back to sorely sting them?"

"I can certainly believe that to be true," the countess said bitterly before she took a deep quaff from her wine glass. Millicent watched her hold the glass by threading her fingers between the stem to hold the body of the glass. Decorum dictated she should not hold anything other than the stem. This time Millicent let it pass, although Lord Fen should be made aware. A sound in the hallway distracted her.

Bryon and Caitlyn walked into the dining room, dressed in their nightgowns. "Papa, I heard a noise," Caitlyn said. "I think it was a horrible ghost. The same one Uncle Fen sees all the time."

Millicent looked at Fen, who seemed properly worried about Caitlyn's words. Maclaevane, however, still smiled. "I shall come to see for myself. And if I find a ghost, I will banish it from the castle."

Bryon moved around the table toward the countess while Caitlyn threw herself into her father's arms.

"Do you like frogs?" he asked the countess.

Millicent pushed back from the table, but not quickly enough. Bryon plopped his bullfrog into the uneaten sorbet in front of the countess and directly across from Millicent.

"How dare you?" the countess screeched as she stared in horror at the frog. Did she mean the frog or the boy? Millicent wasn't certain.

"He's rather difficult to see in green sorbet," Millicent said.

"I hope he doesn't pee in it," Bryon added.

The countess shrieked so loudly, all smiles disappeared at once. Millicent couldn't believe what she'd heard. Bryon needed a swift reprimand. Mentioning a private function of the body was so much worse than putting a frog in the sorbet.

"Remove the frog, Lord Fen," Millicent said as she stood. "Children, you will escort me to the nursery where we will await your father." Millicent turned to Lord Maclaevane. "We'll be upstairs while you look after your guest."

Once she saw the look upon his face, she paused. Lord Maclaevane appeared ready to bolt. Millicent took pity on him. What would her mother do in a similar situation?

As far as it depends on you, choose the pathway of peace. Allow gentleness, kindness, and mercy without hypocrisy guide you in dealing with everyone who comes into your life.

Millicent groaned. She had certainly been hypocritical with the countess. Picking on the woman would make her mother cringe. Especially since Millicent was a pretender of the first order, a counterfeit gentlewoman at the very least.

"Lord Fen, will you take the children upstairs? I will attend to the countess."

She walked around to the countess's side of the table to see spots of sorbet on the woman's sleeve. "Allow me to help." Millicent picked a fresh napkin from the sideboard and dabbed the spots. "We will have this cleaned for you. And if it can't be repaired, Lord McDougal will purchase a new gown to replace yours."

"One like yours?" the woman asked with tears in her eyes. "It *is* beautiful."

Millicent threw a sidelong look to Lord Maclaevane to confirm. "Yes, I think that can be arranged."

"Lord Fen," Millicent said. "Please don't forget the young master's frog. Little frogs must learn their manners also."

"Little?" the countess whimpered.

Millicent sympathized. How painful this evening must have been. "This evening is beyond repair for you, Countess. Perhaps we could plan something special for tomorrow in your honor. Perhaps we could picnic in the gardens if the weather holds true. Could I ask the cook to make something especially to your liking?"

The countess held Millicent's gaze, her clear brown eyes misted with unshed tears. "I have had a singular adoration for sweet coconut cakes ever since Lord Mc-Dougal's cook first made them for me years ago. But in recent years, since I became a countess, she has said she isn't able to make them for lack of the proper ingredients. And she stubbornly refuses to give me the recipe. I miss them."

For years the woman had wanted Lord McDougal's coconut cakes? And not once in all this time she didn't feel free to ask Lord McDougal to intercede on her behalf?

Earlier, upon her arrival, the countess denied she'd asked for food. Could *that* act have meant more than Millicent had originally believed? All during the meal, the countess only picked at her food. Millicent was certain a deeper meaning came into play. Not only about the countess's connection with food, but her understanding with Lord Maclaevane. Millicent decided she must have been mistaken about their relationship or lack of, and it had been a product of the countess's imagination.

"Coconut cakes are my favorite too," Bryon said as Lord Fen gathered the frog. "Cook doesn't care for the taste of coconut and is not interested in them. I shall find you a frog of your own if you get coconut cakes for us, Countess."

The countess gasped. "No, I have no need of a frog."

"Very well done, Countess," Millicent said. "You have managed to salvage Lord McDougal's honor when his table was violated. Even better, you have given everyone something to look forward to in the future."

The countess perked at Millicent's words. Millicent had managed to say the perfect words to raise the countess back to her esteemed position.

"I did?"

"I think we should have coconut cakes daily while the countess is in residence," Lord Maclaevane said. "However, I wonder if anyone who would bring a frog to the table should deserve a special treat."

"Please do not deny him for my sake. Let all be forgiven and forgotten so everyone can look forward to the future." To give her credit, the countess took pity on Bryon.

Millicent felt even guiltier. With a little kindness shown to her, the countess willingly returned the favor to her tormentor. Even to a boy who behaved abominably.

"Fine," Lord Maclaevane announced. "It is settled. Bryon, if you give the countess a formal apology, you'll be allowed to share in the coconut cakes."

"But what about my snake?" Bryon patted his pocket.

Chapter Ten

Only the countess and Millicent remained at the table after everyone else departed. The countess breathed a sigh, sounding much like relief. "I think I handled that well in the end. I always seem to make a fool of myself around that man. I don't know why I continue to bother. It's become a habit I cannot seem to break."

Millicent tried not to frown at her words. "Wonderful decorum under attack, Countess. My—the duchess would give you excellent marks for your charitable recovery."

"The Duchess of Weatherly would think I handled myself well? I never believe I'm doing or saying the right thing. My late husband always said I erred in everything."

Millicent experienced dismay at the countess's revealing comment. They had something in common. Millicent knew well what feeling like a failure could do to a person. Her own brother, Andrew, was a prime example. Andrew did and said the most outrageous things, only to confide later in private he'd wished he'd not done so. Could the countess have a similar problem?

"It's difficult to be sure if one is following proper decorum," Millicent ventured. "Since you have been on the continent, you surely have been subject to any number of different customs."

"You destroyed me at dinner," the countess said and then giggled. "You were bent on bringing me to ruin. Did you think I didn't know?"

Millicent suddenly wanted to flee. "I behaved abominably and your good humor brings me lower than you, showing me for the miserable wretch I am. I am not in the position to reprove anyone since I am the foremost example of a person gone astray from their manners. I humbly beg your forgiveness."

The countess gave a dismissive wave. "You were right in all you said. In truth, I'd rather hear it out loud than to be whispered about behind closed doors. That has happened to me often enough."

Could they find a common ground? Suddenly, Millicent wanted to, and not just for her mother's sake, but because it was the right thing to do. If the countess was willing to meet her halfway, Millicent could put forth the effort. "Table manners are the easiest to make a good show of if you are discerning."

The countess leaned toward Millicent. "Discerning? In what way?"

Millicent smiled. Perhaps she could make amends. "For example. If you find yourself in the company of the Duchess of Weatherly, you would find it impossible to err once you know the secret." Millicent didn't add she could manage to digress even with her mother's pattern to follow. Somehow it seemed easier to show kindness to the poor countess than to herself.

The countess shook her head in denial. "To eat in the presence of the woman known to advise the Queen on matters of etiquette would be my worst nightmare. I couldn't possibly manage." The look of horror on her face told Millicent she believed what she said wholeheartedly.

"If you are attending a formal dinner party, take stock of the invited guests. If you worry about doing or saying the wrong thing, look for a guest you believe has impeccable manners and imitate them. The duchess moves very slowly and deliberately so any who might be unsure can mimic her without being noticed for what they do."

"Like this." Millicent reached slowly for her wine glass, taking care to touch only the stem. After she sipped from the glass, taking care not leave a mark with her lips, Millicent sat it back on the table. The countess watched and then mirrored Millicent.

"No one need even know you are unsure of yourself. Now, on the matter of saying the right thing, I fear I can be no help whatsoever. The only way I succeed in saying the right thing is by saying nothing at all." Millicent recalled sneezing on Lord Finch. "Sometimes I have managed to make a complete muddle without uttering a single word."

The countess laid her napkin on the table. "I have gotten into the nasty habit of attacking first. It is my defense. I have learned some will keep their unkind cuts to a minimum if I show them I am fearless."

"They may not return your cut to your face, but will do so to your back in uncharitable gossip."

The countess nodded. "My ploy didn't work with you. You bested me with ease."

Her remark filled Millicent with regret. "I have been out of sorts and not on my best behavior as of late. I beg your pardon, again."

"And I yours. Now then. Tell me, what do you think about a lady eating too much at a meal?"

"I think it's unwise for anyone to eat to the point of becoming clogged or otherwise encumbered by their food. At my aunt's table, special consideration is given to the vegetable. Dishes prepared with vegetables seem to be less heavy and restrictive."

"Not that way . . . I mean, as in normal eating, just . . ." The countess didn't seem to be able to communicate her thoughts. Millicent's mind went back to the countess's earlier request for food and wondered if she understood.

"I think there is nothing wrong with a lady displaying a healthy appetite. Some people seem to require additional food to sustain them, while others blow up from the smallest portions. Whatever a person's constitution, I think they should be able to enjoy their meals to the fullest possible extent they are able without anyone pointing a finger."

"Even requesting seconds?"

"I wouldn't go *that* far. I would have to know the hostess very well before I requested seconds. It is embarrassing to have a guest make a request which cannot be honored. And requesting seconds can set everything behind. If another course is about to be served, the servants would have to stop and wait for you to finish."

The countess hesitated. "I know some women who do not eat because they think it is unbecoming to have an appetite in front of a member of the opposite sex."

"You *must* eat everything on your plate if at all possible. Do it quietly and without drawing anyone's attention. If you leave food, you risk insulting the hostess."

"While I'm here, may I come to you for advice?"

Millicent silently gulped. She wasn't certain she bought into the act the countess displayed so soon after playing the shrewish adversary.

Seek peace and be the bigger person. Never impugn your own motivations on another individual.

Millicent knew what she needed to do. "With everything I said this evening, what I most failed to say needs to be revealed. To point out anyone's lack of decorum is the very pinnacle of rude behavior. I am deeply ashamed of my conduct."

"Good," the countess said and smiled.

"I have the solution to all our problems," Lord Maclaevane joined from the doorway. He left his hands behind his back in a suspicious manner before he thrust a very familiar dark mahogany volume with gilt lettering into the air.

It could not be happening again! Millicent thought back to the night she decided to quit London. *That* book was the reason she finally had the courage to escape.

"What better way for all of us and especially my children to learn to mind their manners," he said. "I will leave it for you, Lady Mary. Read this and tell us all where we all fall short."

"I would rather eat snails," Millicent said.

"But it's *your* aunt," the countess said. "I like snails in garlic and butter sauce."

Millicent had the idea there wasn't much the countess didn't like to eat, but this time held her tongue.

"Countess Rachessa, I cannot do it," Millicent said. Nothing could have prepared her for the sight of her mother's book in Lord Maclaevane's hands.

"Yes, you most certainly can. What has suddenly happened to all the spunk you so easily displayed earlier?"

"I have learned my lesson."

"I shall lend you a hand. Give me the book, Lord

McDougal. I shall begin reading it in the morning. We can discuss what I've learned at our picnic. It will be great fun."

Lord Maclaevane handed the tome to the countess. "I am suddenly Lord McDougal again, Countess?"

The countess's face came alive with a bright smile and she stood. "I'm attempting to be proper, Maclaevane. I shall retire, so I will be able to rise early and begin anew."

"I'll walk with you." Millicent stood also. The last thing she wanted to do was to talk to Lord Maclaevane about her mother's book.

Lord Maclaevane gave them a deep bow. "I wish you both a good night."

The countess waited for Millicent's response. Millicent wanted to step on his foot. Instead, she walked to stand next to the countess and simply said, "Goodnight, Lord McDougal." She gave him her curtsy.

The countess followed suit and together they made their way down the dark hallway.

"I know I have deplorable manners, and not just with servants," the countess said as they walked. "Remember, I believed you to be a servant. I was my late husband's paid housekeeper before he married me."

Millicent tried not to look as shocked as she felt by the revelation. "Perhaps that is why you seek perfection in everyone around you."

"I don't think so," the countess said with sadness in her voice. "I treat everyone the way my late husband used to treat his servants. Deplorable, isn't it? In a single evening you've shown me the error of my ways. You've set an example for me. If a slip of a girl can be so forgiving at the drop of a hat, I can too. Now you must help me so I can go to London without humiliating myself. With your help, I believe I can do it."

"I've heard rumors you've reached an agreement with Lord McDougal?"

The countess laughed. "I don't really love Maclaevane. He is much too handsome. And those children of his would eat me alive. There is no one else around here to choose from, so I chase after him like a wild tigress. In London, I believe I would fare much better. Besides, Maclaevane wants an English wife, like his first."

"Why do you say so?"

"He's been very vocal about going to London to find a suitable wife and mother for his children. He has even sought the help of a good friend living in London to help in his endeavors."

"Perhaps we shouldn't speak of this." Millicent had no desire to think of Lord Maclaevane with a wife.

"He speaks freely of it. Perhaps because he wanted to dissuade me from my pursuit of him. For a while I was determined to have him as my second husband."

"Oh. Perhaps we should speak of something else."

The countess fanned herself. "I grew up not far from here. Maclaevane and I played together as children. I know I should address him properly, but I fail to think of him as anyone other than the silly boy who put a snake in my knickers. He and young Bryon are just alike."

Millicent thought of her own brothers. "I've had a snake or two in my knickers. Oh! That didn't sound quite proper."

"You are a breath of fresh air, Lady Mary. And I shall call you Mary in private, mannerly or not. I'm glad I behaved badly or I might not have come to know you so well. I will count you as a dear friend from this day forward and there is nothing you can do to stop me."

"I am not the person you believe me to be," Millicent said. When would this end? She didn't deserve this woman's friendship. "This has to end. I'm an imposter."

Having reached the countess's door to her rooms, she pulled Millicent inside and shut the door. "Be quiet, someone will overhear you. I already know your secret. You are not the niece of the Duke and Duchess of Weatherly and it doesn't surprise me. You have too much common sense to be a member of that snooty family. However, I know you come from good quality."

"Is that a compliment?"

The countess placed the book she held on the nightstand and then moved to the mirror. She began to remove pins from her hair. "I think it was. I meant it as one. However, like yours, my mouth doesn't always work the way it should."

Millicent perched on a chair. "Would it surprise you to hear I am their only daughter?"

The countess laughed at Millicent's wit, until she realized Millicent wasn't laughing with her. "You are?"

Millicent nodded. "I came here under the dark shadow of a lie. I didn't want anyone to know I left London after my mother published her book, the very same book you promised to read for Lord McDougal. I claimed to be my own cousin, Mary. And then I feared what I'd do to my mother's reputation once the deception was revealed. I do know this much, I can't keep telling everyone I meet a lie. Nor can I keep making friends and making them part of my conspiracy."

The countess paused and turned away from her reflection. "Perhaps we can say you lost memory of your true identity? I've heard it can happen in rare cases."

"I think loss of memory has something to do with a blow to the head."

The countess grinned. "I could hit you. Trust me, I really could."

Millicent thought for a second. "How would we explain my not having an injury earlier? Also, I confided in both Misses Carter and Sully."

"I have not met your Miss Sully, but I fear I've made an enemy of Miss Carter."

"You must apologize. Miss Carter is a wonderful woman. She is here helping even though she has no desire to stay in the highlands. And look at my hair. No one has ever done my hair so beautifully."

The countess gasped. "She did that? I must make amends immediately."

"Because you feel so contrite?"

"Even more so now you've shared the secret of your hair style. And, I wouldn't want you to get a big head. After all, it will take more than one evening to transform me from a shallow witch into a good friend. I won't have you believing you can work miracles."

Millicent enjoyed their banter, but the seriousness of her dilemma nagged all the while. "I must speak to Lord Maclaevane about what I've done."

"I don't believe Maclaevane would look upon your deception lightly. Men are funny that way. If they discover you've lied once, even if the necessity to conceal the truth was to protect *them*, they never fully trust you again. Even if in the end the lie hurt nobody, except you."

Millicent heard the pain in her voice. She made a promise to herself. If somehow she managed to extricate herself from the tangle of deception she'd created, she would never lie again. Never.

"What if we say you wanted to come to the highlands and were afraid you'd be abducted and held for ransom?"

"That is word for word what my mother's publisher said as he planned my escape."

The countess screamed. "You are an innocent! Do you realize what this means?"

Millicent shook her head. She had no idea what had the countess so excited.

"You are not to blame for the lie. Anyone can see

that. You have been led astray by a gentleman, who by all which is right and just should have known better."

"Sir Henry was only trying to protect my mother's good name. I was to have my first season in polite society. We both feared what I might do to cause my mother shame."

The countess tsk-tsked. "There is good reason to have a season in London and it has nothing to do with finding the best suitor. It would have opened your eyes to what the world is like. You would have learned not all gentlemen are above reproach and I believe this could well be the case with Sir Henry. With more experience you might have realized he didn't seek your best interests. Or those of your mother, for that matter. There are secret motivations at work here I do not believe you have considered."

"So do I tell Lord Maclaevane what I've done?"

Chapter Eleven

Millicent and the countess formulated a plan, and for the first night since she arrived in the highlands, Millicent slept peacefully—until the scream that awakened her, which would be one she'd remember all the days of her life.

Millicent bolted upright in bed. Poor Aphrodite jumped onto her leg and dug in her sharp claws. At the sound of a second bloodcurdling scream, Millicent tucked Aphrodite under her arm, leaped from her bed and paused only a second to throw a wrapper over a single shoulder before she dashed out the door.

A commotion arose in the distance from the direction of the countess's rooms. Before she encountered anyone while in an indecent state of dress, she sat Aphrodite down to shrug into her robe.

When Millicent reached down to pick Aphrodite back up, she discovered her gone. She turned back to see a white streak racing down the dark hallway. Millicent couldn't decide if she should return for a candle or keep going.

"Lady Mary?" a female voice rang out, echoing along the cold walls.

"Victoria? Is that you?"

"Hurry," Victoria said as she rounded the corner holding a lantern high in the air. "Come quickly. It's the countess. I fear she's dead."

Millicent gasped at Victoria's words, but another sound accompanied her inhalation. "What was that?" Millicent asked.

"What?" Victoria questioned as she moved nearer.

"I heard something," Millicent said. She swore they weren't alone.

"I heard nothing save the thunder of my own heart. You must hurry. I fear the worst has happened to the poor woman."

Millicent said no more as she followed Victoria's running gait to the south wing and found the servants milling around her doorway. As she entered the room, she could see the countess's inert body, clad in a thin nightgown, and sprawled lifeless upon the floor.

Millicent rushed into the room, where Lord Maclaevane bent over the countess. "Is she dead?"

Lord Maclaevane reached his hand down to her

throat and leaned closer to place his ear near her mouth. "She is barely breathing, but she's alive."

Millicent looked to Lord Fen over Lord Maclaevane's broad shoulder. "Help get her off the cold floor and into her bed."

Lord Maclaevane needed no help as he swooped her into his arms and took long strides across the floor. The countess's arms hung loose and her head lulled back.

"I'll summon the doctor," Lord Fen said.

"Go, quickly," Lord Maclaevane agreed.

Millicent brought the covers up under the countess's chin and fluffed the pillows under her head. "The countess was screaming before you discovered her like this?"

"Aye," His Lordship said. "Screamed with terror."

"What could have happened?" Millicent asked, but expected no answer. "Stroke the fire, this room is cold. Bring me some tea and see if there are any smelling salts to be found."

Victoria started for the door. "I have some. I bought a bottle before I left Brighton, fearing the worst in the highlands."

Lord Maclaevane motioned to her. "Quickly, Miss Carter. Go get the salts."

"But do not go back to your room alone," Millicent said. "Lord McDougal, please send one of your men with her, and could we light some candles? I do not wish the countess to awaken to this dark." She sat next to the countess and picked up her frail hand. She rubbed it between her own. "She's so cold."

His Lordship moved to stand behind Millicent and placed a hand on her shoulder. Tears stung the back of her eyes.

"Please let her awaken." Millicent placed her hand on Lord Maclaevane's arm.

How long it took for Victoria to return, Millicent didn't know. It seemed an eternity.

Victoria removed the lid and held the tiny vial under the countess's nose.

The countess gasped.

"She's alive," Victoria whispered.

"W-what? W-why are you h-here? What happened?"

"Stay calm, Countess," Millicent said. "We hoped you could tell us what happened. You screamed twice and then we discovered you cold upon your floor, dressed only in thin silk."

"I remember. I saw a ghost. A most frightening specter, white as snow. Bigger than Lord Fen."

Millicent looked around the room and saw nothing resembling a big, white Lord Fen. "Were you asleep, before you saw it?"

The countess shook her head. "I was reading your— the duchess's book. Then the light flickered on my candle. I looked up and it filled the doorway weaving to and fro. Did it come to reveal my death?"

Millicent started to protest when Lord Maclaevane stepped forward. "In the highlands, we have many who believe in the *second sight*. Did you see a face on your specter?"

Victoria looked at Millicent, who shrugged.

"Nay, I saw only white."

"Milord," one of the men called out from the doorway, "we found this in the hallway." The man held out a white sheet and a thick broomstick.

Millicent walked with Lord Maclaevane to examine what the man found. "Where are the children?" she asked and watched him dash away in search of them. She tried to follow, but soon fell behind.

He was on his way back from the nursery when she met him. "They're gone," he told her. "The children have run away."

Millicent didn't want to believe it. "We should have been more concerned about their pranks."

Lord Maclaevane's face told her he didn't care for her words. "I blame myself for not being stricter with them. Bryon is so young. Why would I imagine he would do this?"

Millicent shook her head. "I wasn't thinking of Bryon. I don't believe any of the pranks were his idea. I remember believing at the time Caitlyn coached him. I fear they may believe they've killed the countess."

"Why?"

"I heard a noise in the hall, when Miss Carter came for me. She told me the countess was dead. I think perhaps the children were coming to my room and they heard Miss Carter's words."

Lord Maclaevane threaded his fingers through his loose hair. "If Caitlyn believes she is responsible for someone's death, there is no telling what she'll do."

"Could she have run away again?"

His Lordship's lack of response spoke volumes. "She would not take Bryon with her. The last time she ran away, she promised to never take Bryon with her again. Sadly, I couldn't get her to agree to not do something so foolish herself."

"Where could they be?" Millicent questioned, knowing he had no answer.

"I need to alert the household."

Millicent wanted to help. "What can I do?"

"Gather everyone in the main hall. We need to organize a search."

The halls were too dark to move about with ease, and Millicent walked back to the countess's room to find the housekeeper. "Lord McDougal wants everyone to congregate in the main hall. The children are missing. And have someone light the lamps in the castle. All of them."

Millicent went back to her rooms to dress properly. The dress she'd worn earlier in the day hung over the dressing screen. Out of habit, her modesty dictated dressing behind the screen. As she walked nearer the sound of a sob jolted her. The children?

Bryon sat on a footstool behind the screen with his face buried in his hands. "I thought you would never come," he sobbed. "Caitlyn said I had to wait for you here. She made me promise. Did we kill the countess?"

Millicent reached down and pulled him into her arms. "The countess will be fine. Where is Caitlyn?"

"She's gone," he sobbed.

"Did she tell you where she was going?"

"No, she was crying. She said she had to leave forever because she is a barbarian."

Bryon's words cut deeply into her heart, and she didn't know if she'd ever be the same. Caitlyn was running, just as Millicent had. "She said nothing else?"

"Only for me to stay here and wait for you. Caitlyn said you would take care of me. Does that mean she isn't coming back?" Bryon sobbed louder after his question showed Millicent he believed his sister intended to never return.

She fought the rising tide of panic. The thought of a small girl alone in the highlands couldn't be sanely borne for long. It was too painful to consider. What would Lord Maclaevane do if he failed to find her? "Come, we must find your father and let him know what is happening."

Millicent gave him another hug before she urged him to move. "We must show your father you are safe."

She took his little hand in hers and guided him toward the door. Before her fingers touched the latch the door began to swing open.

"Lady Mary, I'm so sorry! I didn't mean to kill the countess." Caitlyn threw herself at Millicent, who managed to hold both crying children. However, once Aphrodite entered the fray, Millicent found herself flat on her backside with the children tumbling about her.

"Caitlyn," Bryon howled. "You came back."

"I'm sorry. I only wanted to scare her. To make her go away."

"The countess is not dead, Caitlyn."

"Yes, she is. I heard Miss Carter tell you she's dead. I killed her."

"No," Millicent insisted. "Miss Carter was mistaken. The countess only fainted. I promise you."

"Are you certain?"

Millicent nodded. "The countess will be fine. Right now we must let your father know you are safe."

"I can see for myself." The sound of Lord Maclaevane's voice came from the doorway. After Millicent looked up into his eyes, she could no longer be strong. A wrenching sob bubbled from deep in her breast and broke free.

Caitlyn seemed to panic from Millicent's tears. "Is the countess alive?" While she still clung tight to Millicent, Caitlyn reached her hand toward her father.

Lord Maclaevane came to join the three of them on the floor. His face was pinched into a grimace holding only a hint of the joy he must feel to see his children safe. He cradled them both against his chest while Millicent tried to extract herself from her unladylike sprawl on the floor.

"Yes, she is fine now. Warm and cozy in her bed."

Millicent realized her robe had become pinned underneath the children and she couldn't move. It was suddenly more than she could handle. More tears followed.

"Then why is Lady Mary crying?" Caitlyn asked and hid her face in her father's shoulder.

"I'm sorry," Millicent managed to get out.

Lord Maclaevane groaned and moved with his children still attached to put a free arm about Millicent's shoulder. She buried her wet face against the thick woolen plaid scarf like the one he'd sacrificed the night they'd met. The warmth of the wool, his firm grip, and a delicious spicy scent entered her thoughts to give her relief and at the same time cause a different kind of chaos inside her.

"Why are you crying, Lady Mary?" she heard Caitlyn ask.

"I believe you are witnessing tears of joy for your safe return," Lord Maclaevane said to his daughter. Millicent nodded in the comfort of his strong grip. It was so good to be held by him. Better than good. It was unlike anything she'd ever experienced. When she heard Lord Maclaevane's raspy voice followed by a near sob of his own, Millicent forced herself to calm down before she unmanned him.

Lord Maclaevane cleared his throat. "I fear my dear, Caitlyn, you must be punished for your foolish prank. Your behavior is beyond the pale. Although the countess will survive your attack, if you had played this trick on someone with a weaker constitution, the result could have been far worse."

"I know," Caitlyn squeaked. "I won't complain, even if you refuse to allow me to ride for as long as I live."

Poor Lord Maclaevane. "Could we allow the countess to set her punishment? She has suffered the most harm." Millicent progressed beyond the point of tears, but not beyond wanting to remain within Lord Maclaevane's strong arms. He made no move to pull away from her, so she stayed.

Caitlyn started to cry again. "I don't want you to marry the countess, Papa."

Lord Maclaevane's face twisted in puzzlement. "Is that why you tried to scare the countess? I have no intention of marrying the countess. Not now or ever."

His words thrilled Millicent even though she'd already suspected as much.

"Papa, I heard you tell the countess you wished to be married."

Lord Maclaevane smiled. "Yes, I told the countess I was seeking a wife. I also informed her I would not marry until I found someone who could be a mother to my children. In that regard, the countess does not suit me."

"Why can't you marry our Lady Mary?" Caitlyn demanded while she swiped her tears with the backs of her hands.

Millicent couldn't meet his eyes. She could feel her face color as she considered what his answer would be to his near hysterical daughter. He hugged Millicent closer against his hard chest and she nearly swooned.

"I think it would be splendid to be married to Lady Mary. She would make a fine wife and no doubt an even more wonderful mother. You both have proven her value to you by seeking her assistance in a time of dire need. . . . But perhaps she won't have me." He released her and took great pains to extract his children from her with the utmost decorum.

Millicent wished he wasn't such a gentleman.

Caitlyn sobbed again and turned to her. "Will you, Lady Mary? Will you marry Papa?"

"Will you marry us?" Bryon asked.

Where was her wit when she needed it most?

Chapter Twelve

Millicent handled all of the castle's affairs until the day of the dinner party without a single insurmountable problem to plague her. However, handling her growing attraction to Lord Maclaevane became another matter altogether. All he had to do was enter the same room to send her heart into a flutter and her stomach into a tight clench.

True to form, Millicent wisely used each occasion to humiliate herself further. Whether it was spilling, ripping, tripping, or falling, she did it all and often.

"What has come over you?" the countess asked as they gathered to make centerpieces for the table. "If you continue like this we will not have enough ribbon to finish. If I didn't know better I'd say you've taken one of Cupid's arrows to the heart."

Millicent grew warm at the countess's suggestion.

Victoria looked up from the bundle of autumn leaves, peacock feathers, and dried ivy, as she secured it with a bright orange bow. She watched the two of them with undisguised interest.

A blush came over Millicent. "Please, countess, no more talk of love."

Victoria held a new piece of ribbon to her. "What is it? Have you gone and swallowed a pin?"

Tears started flowing out of Millicent's eyes faster than her discreet handkerchief could mop them away.

"Millicent, you are scaring us," the countess demanded. "Whatever is wrong with you?"

"Will you two take care someone doesn't hear you call me Millicent? I believe Lord Maclaevane may have asked me to marry him and I didn't say yes. Now he won't even look at me."

"What?" the countess screamed. "Tell."

Victoria harrumphed. "If you ask me, he does little else but look at you from morning until night. Since when must a lord take tea each day in the nursery? He's positively besotted with you."

Millicent didn't wish to speak of the melancholy surrounding her heart, but the faces of her friends demanded an account. "In all my years, I've never once considered marrying. Well . . . I once imagined wedding a dashing highlander I'd made up in my mind. I promise that was the only time I entertained the notion. Now it seems I think of little else."

"There, there," the countess said calmly. "If you want to wed the man, simply tell him so. The worst he could do is tell you no. He refused me, and frankly it wasn't as difficult for me as one might imagine."

"Countess!" Victoria snapped.

The countess seemed genuinely surprised by Victoria's stern tone. "What did I say wrong?"

Victoria placed her hand upon her hip and wagged a finger at the countess. "She cannot want to hear you've asked the man she loves to marry *you*, Countess."

"She didn't love him then. Did you?"

Millicent dropped her leaves and buried her face in her hands. "Love? Stop," she moaned. "This is not helping. It's only making me feel more dreadful. I don't think I'll ever be the same. Why didn't someone have the courtesy to inform me about these miserable forces warring in my heart? I would have moved heaven and earth to avoid them completely."

"I told you," Victoria said to the countess.

"Fine," the countess snapped back. "However, I think Millicent is making too much of this. His Lordship is well worth catching. It's good for a woman to have strong feelings for a man who has declared his intentions for her."

The countess moved closer and leaned toward Millicent. "Do you not read of love in all those books you bury your face in both day and night?"

She heaved a sigh. "On the contrary, I have read of love where the result was ruination and despair. I read nothing of this panic roiling within my person. Or if I did—I failed to understand the true meaning of it. One minute I'm elated to have discovered love and the next I'm heart-sick he does not feel the same."

"Forgive me," Victoria said in a hushed tone. "I have never been in love so I can't help you."

"Love's effect is different for all, so no one can help you, my dear," the countess said, sounding as if she understood love's mysteries well.

Victoria huffed. "Perhaps Lady Mil—Mary doesn't want to hear there is no help for her ailment, Countess."

The countess blinked her expressive brown eyes. "Have I erred again, Victoria? You should not have allowed me to go on. Didn't we agree a condition of your employment would be to help me control my wayward tongue?"

Victoria huffed. "In that case, I think you need to raise my wages."

The countess wrinkled her nose and appeared perplexed. "It was only yesterday I persuaded you to work for me, Victoria. You already have determined I am paying you too little?"

Victoria gave her bow a final tug and held her arrangement up to be admired before she answered. "If I am to be held responsible for your speech, I need to be compensated. Your hair is much easier tamed into submission."

"Point taken. For heaven's sake, I take it back then.

My wayward hair is infinitely more important than my mouth."

The countess looked to Millicent, who shook her head to silently communicate the countess's error.

"Well, all right then," the countess sulked. "You shall have your raise."

Mentally applauding the countess's capitulation, Millicent patted her hand. "Well done, Countess. Victoria will take good care of you. And you will never want for a more agreeable and honorable confidant."

Victoria reached across the table and patted Millicent's hand. "Thank you, Lady Mary. Now back to your dreadful ailment."

"Ailment?" Lord Maclaevane called out as he entered the room and took them by surprise. "Please forgive me, I couldn't help overhearing. Have you taken ill, Lady Mary? Allow me to send for the doctor."

The countess stood and smoothed the wrinkles in her skirt. "The doctor's already here. Did you forget he arrived as your guest only yesterday, Lord McDougal?"

"Right." Lord Maclaevane appeared to be in a fluster when his eyes shifted and he didn't look at Millicent again. "I shall fetch him immediately then."

They'd caused this with their silly talk of love, but neither of her friends spoke in her defense. "I have no need of a doctor."

After both women shrugged, Millicent decided to make an argument. "Lord Maclaevane, you've misunderstood Miss Victoria. She speaks of an entirely different matter. One that would not require a doctor at all."

"Ahem." Lord Maclaevane cleared his throat.

Millicent realized how her words might be perceived and winced. Only the truth would suffice now. "We were speaking of love."

"Well done," the countess said and waved a peacock feather in the air.

"Love?" Lord Maclaevane asked. "Surely you do not view such a tender emotion as an ailment?"

"We were speaking of the transfer of your affections from me to Lady Mary," the countess said out of the blue.

"Countess!" Victoria barked.

"I know. You wish another raise? Perhaps I could just give you a couple of quid each time I err?"

Millicent couldn't look at Lord Maclaevane. "At that rate you would soon be in the poor house, Countess."

"And what has Lady Mary said about my affections for her?" Lord Maclaevane asked with a smile across his entirely too-handsome face. Millicent wanted to dash from the room and hide beneath her bed.

"I have said naught of your affections for me, since you have not declared them."

"I have not?" Lord Maclaevane raised a questioning brow. "Indeed. How foolish of me. I should make amends and do so immediately."

"Lord Maclaevane, please," Millicent pleaded. "This is unseemly. What would you have people think of us? Of me?"

"Let's see, in the past fortnight I've heard all sorts of words bandied about. Besotted, crazed, infatuated, smitten, and love-struck are some of the words I've heard applied to *my* unfortunate condition. In truth, I much prefer head-over-heels in love."

For a moment Millicent felt she might swoon. Heavens, she'd never fainted once! The floor swayed underneath her feet. "What is happening—"

"You have done quite enough, Your Lordship!" Millicent heard Victoria say angrily. She opened her eyes to see the ceiling of her bedroom.

"See there, she's awake. Be gone with you, before you do more damage to the lady's tender sensibilities," the countess demanded.

Millicent turned at the sound of her door easing shut. "What has happened?"

"You have fainted, of course," Victoria said as she began to fluff the pillow under Millicent's head.

The countess moved closer and leaned over Millicent. "You are young. His Lordship should have known better. He's the most eligible bachelor in all of Scotland, despite his unfortunate children. He should not have taken such liberties with his words. He should have eased slowly into his bold declaration."

Millicent remembered. *Head-over-heels in love!* "Surely he's mistaken."

The countess huffed. "Come now, the man knows his own mind. Depend upon it."

Victoria held her hand to Millicent's forehead. "Perhaps we should speak of something else. I have no desire to see you faint again."

"I fainted? Surely not."

"It was the most romantic thing I've ever seen. You should have seen the look on Lord McDougal's face. I think you may have scared years off of his life."

"Serves him right," Victoria sniped. "He shouldn't have spoken so boldly."

The countess sat on the edge of the bed and began to pet Aphrodite. "Where is your heart, Victoria? I have never witnessed a more romantic moment in my life. I shall write about it in my journal so I might always remember. Perhaps one day, I too shall have the good fortune to have love declared to me in such a grand manner. Perhaps I might even faint just like our sweet Millicent did. It's so very romantic."

"This is not the stuff of which sonnets are penned," Victoria insisted. "Lord McDougal should have hid his regard and shared it in a more appropriate setting when they were alone. And you must stop calling her Millicent. She needs to be the one to reveal the truth of her true identity."

"Twaddle, Victoria, if a man cannot be a fool for love, what is this world coming to? I think it's charming."

"I fainted because he declared his love for me?" Millicent said and her stomach cut loose with a terrifying noise which startled both women.

"When did you last eat?" the countess demanded.

"You didn't eat a bite last evening, once Lord McDougal came to the table dressed in all his finery."

Millicent groaned. She couldn't remember when she'd last taken a full meal. With the excitement of guests arriving at all hours and the grand party being only a single day hence, there was little wonder her appetite waned.

"I can't remember," she admitted.

The countess murmured a very rude word. "Doctors! The man wanted to bleed you. He could have destroyed you."

Head-over-heels in love! His words took her breath away.

Head-over-heels in love! Could it be true?

Millicent's stomach protested again. The countess was not far wrong in saying Millicent ignored her food in favor of watching Lord Maclaevane. For an unknown reason, he grew more attractive daily. She wanted to do little else but look at him.

Victoria stepped back. "I'll have the housekeeper send up a tray. Perhaps some tea and scones?"

"With honey and lots of creamy butter," the countess added. "And some caramel pudding. No, wait. Are there leftover pigeons stewed with mushrooms? Maybe the cook still has Millicent's portion since she didn't eat it last evening."

Millicent gazed down to the end of the bed. "You finished it for me, Countess."

The countess sighed and pulled Aphrodite onto her

lap. "Right. I had forgotten. Then perhaps a hearty beef soup and a gooseberry tart or two?"

"Or a dozen?" Victoria groused before she dashed off.

"There now," the countess said. "We will put an end to this malady from which you suffer. A few bites of food will put you right."

"Is that all then?" Millicent's sarcasm was lost upon the countess. "I wish you would have shoved food in my mouth days ago, were it that easy."

A smile spread across the countess face. "I cannot wait to see what transpires at dinner. It follows to be entertaining and maybe even romantic."

"Countess, have you forgotten? I have yet to share my transgressions with Lord Maclaevane. Once I confront him with my behavior, I'm in danger of losing his affection."

"Twaddle," the countess cried.

"I feel certain of it. It would have been better if I had not allowed it to go on so long. I've misled him."

Millicent looked to the doorway in time to see a smile disappear from Lord Maclaevane's face.

"My pardon, Lady Mary. I only thought to see to your improvement," he said with a curt bow before he walked away.

"I spoke too soon," Maclaevane said to his brother. "Again, I have made a disaster of it."

Fen huffed. "Are you certain she has no feelings for you?"

"She said she has misled me. That she should have not allowed it go on so long. What else am I to think?"

"It's too late to turn back now. You love her. Buckle down, Maclaevane, you must find a way to win your lady's heart."

"I cannot win what is not mine to have. Perhaps she has settled her hopes on another. Perhaps *you,* Fen? She seems genuinely taken with you."

"Impossible. She has only words of brotherly kindness for me. It is something else keeping her from surrendering her heart to you."

"Perhaps. After her arrival at McDougal Castle, she hinted of a personal indiscretion on her part. Perhaps she cannot make free with her affections until her err of common sense, as she put it, is put to rest."

"That's it then. I'm certain of it. You have to give her the privacy to speak without worry of being cut short. You have had little time to give her."

"I think you may have it backward. It is she who has had no time for me."

"Do something about it. You are in charge around here. Make time alone with your lady."

Maclaevane laughed heartily before he clapped his brother upon the shoulder. "You realize if Lady Mary accepts me, you will have to become friends with her cat."

Chapter Thirteen

The last thing Millicent wished was to sit down to Lord Maclaevane's dinner party while the black cloud of her deception lingered over her head. A moment longer and she would surely go mad. Tomorrow would be too late. She needed to speak with Lord Maclaevane before the castle became overrun by guests. Already the table had grown from four to six settings. The doctor and his wife made a party of six.

The countess was in rare form, starting from the second she floated through the door on Lord Fen's arm. She chatted on about one matter or another, without the slightest hesitation. After Millicent was called upon for an answer to a question she'd neglected to hear, she took a guess. The delighted peals of laugher from the countess made her wonder if she'd managed to play the fool.

"Let us strike hands to our pledge," the countess said gleefully.

"Wait, perhaps I heard incorrectly," Millicent said.

"I trust you did, since you have agreed to accompany me to India and ride an elephant through the streets of Nepal."

"Forgive me, Countess." Millicent took a drink before she continued. "I fear I must resolve other matters, here in the highlands, before I can commit to such a lengthy journey."

"I am jesting, silly. I asked you to join me in the gardens tomorrow for some quiet time before the remainder of the guests arrive and there will be no time for us to relax and talk. Perhaps Lord McDougal would care to join us?"

"There is so much to be done," Millicent said. "I'm not ready for tomorrow to come."

"I declare," the countess huffed. "You must slow down and take care. We cannot have you fainting again, now can we?"

At the mention of her feminine indiscretion and how it was brought on, Millicent grew warm.

"Do you need some air, Lady Mary?" Lord Fen asked as he started to wave his large hand in front of her face.

"Please no, I am fine."

"I insist," Lord Maclaevane interrupted and directed a comment to her for the first time that evening. "The countess has told me you are not eating well."

"If I take fresh air right now, I fear I'll miss the first course. Which would you have me do?" Her words came out much stronger than she intended.

Lord Maclaevane raised a dark brow and tapped his well-formed fingers upon the table before he remembered his manners and removed his hand. "Forgive me, you are right."

"You cannot be expected to walk about without first eating your meal," the countess said.

"Of course, Countess," Lord Maclaevane said and then signaled for the food to be served.

Never could Millicent have imagined what Lord Maclaevane had planned for their evening repast. At first she failed to catch on to his ploy. The meal started with soup made with chopped spinach and onion, and then onward to fillets of sole in delicate white sauce, potatoes au gratin, roasted duck, orange sauce, asparagus, goose pies in tangy tomato sauce, potted cheese, leg of lamb, mint sauce, green peas, beans aux francais, and of course thick crusty bread with creamy butter. To top it all off, Millicent found herself plied with mince pie, plum tart with cream, rice meringue, and iced pudding fruit.

Once the last cart with tea and nuts was rolled into the room after almost two hours, Millicent cried off. She'd only taken the smallest of helpings, but even that became too much. "One more bite and I am in serious breach of decorum. I think I'll take a stroll."

"I would only be too delighted to escort you, Lady Mary," Lord Maclaevane said as he stood with her.

Since she was already on her feet, she had little recourse. She could hardly feign hunger nor did she want to attempt to sit back down. "Lord Maclaevane." She curtsied and prayed she wouldn't belch.

"I would go with you, but I need to allow my food time to settle." The countess looked positively contented. The image of Aphrodite after a tasty meal was very similar to the expression on the countess's face.

Lord Maclaevane offered his arm and they began a stroll through the length of the drawing room. While they remained within sight of the others, it seemed almost too intimate to Millicent.

"Did you get enough to eat?" Lord Maclaevane lowered his voice so only she could hear, and Millicent breathed a sigh of relief.

"You are very kind to worry about my welfare. I had more than enough."

Lord Maclaevane paused. "I was relieved to hear you had not fainted because of me. I must admit. It was not how I imagined you'd react to my declaration of love."

Millicent shivered from head to toe. "And how did you picture it? I cannot pretend to have knowledge of matters of the heart." The breathless quality of her voice made her look down at her slippers. Why couldn't she speak? What about this man reduced her to wondering if her stockings were set neatly and if she smelled of the garlic in the roasted duck? Everything had changed.

"I pictured us walking through my overgrown gardens with the autumn colors highlighting your rich mahogany hair as it escaped your bonnet. I would turn to you." Lord Maclaevane stopped to face her. He reached for her hand. "I pictured taking your trembling hand in mine."

Millicent gasped at the touch of his hand upon hers. It was the first time she'd been touched by a man in a declaration of love. And it did tremble . . . how could he know?

Lord Maclaevane lifted her hand and bowed over it, bending low from the waist. For a moment, she imagined he intended to kiss it. Her heart fluttered in her chest, but he stopped to look up into her eyes.

The moment seemed an eternity passing before them.

"I pictured myself going down on one knee."

Millicent gasped again as he did just so.

"I pictured myself asking for this lovely hand, to be pledged to mine for all eternity. Lady Mary, will you do me the inestimable honor of becoming my bride?"

A smile stretched her face until it would give no quarter. "Yes!"

"At last!" he shouted.

Millicent's great joy was so brief as to be imagined before she remembered decorum.

Sacred decorum.

"You haven't asked my father for his permission."

Lord Maclaevane's face twisted in confusion. He opened his mouth and then snapped it shut again. He took a deep breath and stood. "But your father is deceased and you have no brothers. Should I have first asked your mother?"

Millicent was well and truly caught. Only the truth would set her free from her self-made trap. "My father is alive and well. I also claim five brothers all living, although I cannot attest as to how well. According to my mother, they are heathens. Of the first order, as Caitlyn would put it."

Lord Maclaevane seemed at first flummoxed, before his face darkened. Millicent prayed he would not give way to anger. "You are the only daughter of the Duke and Duchess of Weatherly?"

Her unspeakable humiliation made her weak in the knees. "So it would seem."

Judged by the looks of his two brows pulled tight into one, Lord Maclaevane's anger grew. "You are Lady Millicent Wainright, daughter of the Duke and Duchess of Weatherly, of whom has been settled the tidy sum of one-hundred thousand pounds?"

Millicent winced at the figure named for her bride price. All of London spoke of it. It hadn't occurred to her that the news had traveled as far as the highlands of Scotland. "One and the same."

"I withdraw my claim," Lord Maclaevane said.

Millicent didn't expect to hear him cry off. Not that! "Too late. You are caught."

"Then so are you," he said before he pulled her into his arms. She only had a moment to wonder his intent before he kissed her. At first hard and unyielding, his kiss seemed meant for punishment. A second later, he softened his lips in an inviting assault of pleasure. Millicent reached up to throw her arms about his neck. Then, just as suddenly he released her and stomped off without a glance over his shoulder.

Taking solace in her bedroom, Millicent stared at the countess who stood next to Victoria. Both appeared ill at ease and somber. How did everything go so wrong? "Tell him, I release him from his pledge of marriage. I don't know why I dared to tell him he was caught. The words came out of my mouth before I could stop them."

The countess reached out to hug Millicent. "Do not think of yourself so unkindly. He will get over it. If he is head over heels as he proclaims, he will find a way to forgive you. We all were witness to the way he kissed you. Trust me. You will be forgiven."

At the sound of a knock, Millicent jumped internally. Victoria went to the door. It was Mrs. McDuffy with a large tray in her hands.

"Lord McDougal had to go down the hill to the villagers. But first he bade me to deliver a tray for you. He feared you would not break your fast since you refused the morning gong."

The countess released Millicent to see to the tray. "See there. He has forgiven you already."

Millicent couldn't stop the worry anymore than she could cease loving him. "When did he say he'd be returning?"

The housekeeper helped the countess make room for the tray. "He didn't say. One of the villager's children took a fall. He is taking the doctor to see about the child. He asks if you would look after Caitlyn and Bryon in case he's delayed. He did mention you should not fear he would be late for the dinner party this evening."

"Thank you so much for the food, Mrs. McDuffy. Has Lord Fen gone too?"

"Yes, and you are welcome, milady. Please send for me if you need anything."

"Thank you."

Millicent watched the countess approach the food after the housekeeper left the room. "You should not question Lord Maclaevane's regard for you ever again. He has sent you coconut cakes! I shall ask Mrs. McDuffy to send more, straight away."

"One lump or two, Laird McDougal?"

Maclaevane looked up at the kindly face and shook his head. "None, Mrs. McKinley." He normally took two, but he would not take from the mouths of those entrusted to his care. The small cottage had many improvements done as of late, but still the family of four would not have sugar to spare.

"We're honored ye come along with the doctor when ye did," the woman said before she went back to the corner where the doctor tended her injured son.

Fen rubbed his hands together over the hearth of the peat fire. "Have you decided to forgive her?"

"There is nothing to forgive, Fen."

"You'll send her away then?"

"Away?" Maclaevane sipped the bitter tea, glad of its warmth if nothing else. "Nonsense, Fen. For years, I believed I'd never find someone to capture my heart. Now after finding the very thing I questioned even existed, do you think I'd let her escape my clutches?"

"I thought you were angry with her deception?"

"You are mistaken. Lady Millicent does not have a deceitful bone in her body. It was not her deception. The countess told me how it transpired. It seems her mother's publisher placed the notion of coming to the highlands in her beautiful head.

"More than placed in her head, the scoundrel saw to all the arrangements himself. Then he sent her off without a chaperone. It's a wonder vagabonds didn't set upon her and take her for ransom."

"The man should be horsewhipped," Fen said in disgust. "Are we going to London any time soon? I'll be glad to take care of the publisher while you speak to Lady Milli's father."

"The Duke of Weatherly is likely to have me drawn and quartered, since I have already asked for her hand without first gaining his permission. True to form, I have given them a reason to speak badly of our highland manners. Not to mention what the gossipmongers will make of her staying with us without a proper chaperone."

"Now I'm beginning to understand. Unless we get this publisher fellow to speak up, you are in a bit of a spot. You may even be viewed as a bounder."

"So it would seem. Worst of all, I have no idea of how Lady Millicent views my assault on her person."

Fen huffed. "It was a kiss, not an assault."

Maclaevane wasn't so sure. He'd kissed her soundly and enjoyed it more than he could imagine. "How she views it, remains to be seen."

Fen eased down into the only other chair in the tiny cottage. After the chair creaked under his weight, he jumped back up. "You have one thing in your favor."

"What is that?"

"You asked for Lady Millicent without knowledge of the fortune which comes with her hand in marriage. Any father worth his salt would want that for his daughter."

"My dear brother, you also forget how the woman must worry about her fortune."

Fen shrugged. "I do not ken how that would matter. The money will make life easier at McDougal Castle for her and everyone. She can entertain and do as she wills with it. The children will be pleased."

"You don't understand my dilemma. If I should forgive her too quickly after learning she comes with a fortune, she will question my motives. It must be difficult for her to believe a man would not find her dowry tempting."

"Right," Fen agreed, but Maclaevane didn't know if he understood.

"It will be hard enough for her to become a mother to half-grown children. To add additional burdens to the pot may make her reconsider. You know the blasted money means nothing to me. However, she may think otherwise based on her experience among the idle ton."

Fen moved to stand next to the fire. "Do you think she wanted to leave London to take herself off the market?"

"Can you imagine the number of offers she has received? The poor duke must have installed a new-fangled revolving door to keep them in an orderly line."

"I don't envy your conversation with the Duke of Weatherly. Having his daughter come up missing will no doubt affect his disposition. Maybe you should start with the mother and work your way up."

"I have a much better place to start. I have the confidence of the best source imaginable to gain access into Weatherly Hall. Lady Millicent's brother has tried for the past two years to get me to throw my name into the hat."

"Very fortunate for you."

"Her brother is Lord Andrew Wainright, or as you so

often called him in the past, 'that blamed, blackguard merry-Andrew who needs a good thrashing or two.'"

"No!" Fen cried. "It slipped my mind he is Lady Millicent's brother. Talk about the black sheep. She is a saint next to him."

"He's not nearly so bad. You only chafe because he bested you in front of your friends and family."

Fen started to pace about the small room. "None of that. Unfair. How could I foresee the merry-Andrew could find his way around the deck of a ship so well when he was raised in polite society? I thought he was a dandy."

"That should teach you to wager what you don't care to lose."

"The *Princess Ellen* was my best ship. He uses her as a toy."

"From the rumors I've heard, Lord Andrew has become a hero of sorts. He's captured two pirate ships in the last month and freed a maiden held for ransom. If everything proceeds as I pray it will, you'll be related by marriage, Fen. Perhaps you'll have the opportunity to win the *Princess Ellen* back."

"Do you think so?"

Maclaevane shrugged. "It's possible. Lord Andrew will be pleased to have me wed his sister. He'll believe it was all his idea and may be generous because of it."

"What did he tell you about Lady Millicent when he tried to interest you in her?"

"Lord Andrew didn't tell me this, but I've heard rumors Lady Millicent's brothers spoiled her shamelessly. No wonder she got on so well with Caitlyn. Lady Millicent could climb a tree before she could walk."

Fen laughed. "You don't say. Aye, then she will fit in well here."

"Now I only need to find a way to stay away from her until I can speak to her father of my honorable intentions."

Chapter Fourteen

Millicent walked into the dining room on Lord Mc-
Dougal's arm, his very rigid arm. When he hesitated to
offer it, she nearly died of mortification. It was no more
than she deserved, but still, it hurt to have him shun her.

His equally expressionless face told her nothing of
what he felt for her since she openly admitted her deception. From the time he'd returned from the village,
he refused to give her a second to explain how she had
come to throw sand in his eyes. It promised to be a long
evening.

Millicent tried to take comfort from all her hard
work. The dinner party turned out better than she imagined. The table linens Mrs. McDuffy produced were the
most beautiful she'd ever seen. Millicent cringed to use
them. They used gold-plated chargers under the fragile

porcelain service from Limoges, France. The fifty plates Millicent found stashed in a box had been a wedding present to Lord Maclaevane's first wife. Caitlyn insisted the plates with picturesque games birds edged with Roman gold were perfect for the occasion and Millicent agreed.

It was to be a twelve-course meal with ices to cleanse the pallets in between. Mrs. McDuffy assured Millicent she had not served all the food the night before so all promised to proceed without chaos.

After Lord Maclaevane welcomed his guests, he thanked Millicent for all her hard work. He even managed to sound fond of her as he spoke of his appreciation of her contributions to the success of the evening.

No sooner had he signaled for the meal to be served than a commotion could be heard coming from the front of the castle.

For a second, Millicent swore she heard her father's angry voice.

"The Duke and Duchess of Weatherly request Lord McDougal's presence," one of His Lordship's men came to announce only seconds later.

"Where is she? What have you done with her?"

Millicent looked up to see her father towering in the doorway. As far as decorum went, this far exceeded a sneeze.

"Not now dear," came another familiar voice. Millicent's father stepped aside and the duchess moved around him. She curtsied to Lord Maclaevane. "My humble apologies for our lack of promptness."

Both Lord Fen and the countess took the duchess's words for a cue to move to the opposite end of the table. Millicent needed to give them high marks for the courteous gesture. Then she remembered the countess saying she never wanted to find herself at the same table with the Duchess of Weatherly. So generosity, on both their parts, probably was more fear than anything else.

Millicent was accustomed to a quick burst of bluster from her father with little else to follow. He was always more than content to allow his wife to set forth the discipline. He would let her mother handle everything from that point forward. Millicent knew her mother would do or say nothing until they were alone. However, Lord Maclaevane could not know this. From the look on his handsome face, he was uncertain what to do or say.

Millicent rose to greet her parents and extended her hand to her mother. Millicent knew her mother oft cautioned about affection in the public eye, however she'd missed them so much. "We were about to be served, but may I delay for an embrace?"

Her mother reached for her and she flew into the comfort of the arms that meant more than life to her. How she'd missed this. Tears dampened her eyes, but she managed to stay them off.

"Your father and I have missed you," her mother whispered into Millicent's ear.

"No more than I have missed the both of you."

Her father seated her mother in the place recently vacated by the countess and took the chair next to Millicent, but hesitated. He'd never hugged Millicent in public. When he reached for her, the tears she held at bay came pouring out. She buried her face against his chest until she had control.

"Your mother and I missed you."

"Yes, Father. I shall find a way to make it right."

With decorum restored, the meal continued. Millicent could see her mother take note of how her daughter handled the affair. As luck would have it, they went through eleven of the twelve courses without a single hurdle. Her mother beamed with pride. For the first time, Millicent relaxed and began to enjoy herself as she sat next to them.

While her father didn't downright refuse to speak with Lord Maclaevane, there was tension between them. Still in all, under the circumstances, Millicent took pride in her accomplishments.

The trouble with luck was, one could lose it in a hair's breadth of time. From down at the far end of the table Lord Fen let out a high-pitched scream, shattering a piece of stemware.

Like a house of cards, waves of screams both male and female alike tumbled down the table toward Millicent.

"Aphrodite is still alive and well, I see," Millicent's father muttered.

"Your Grace," her mother warned the duke in the singular tone Millicent knew well.

Millicent looked down to see Aphrodite leading her family of baby mice on an outing. They marched in formation behind her until they all reached Millicent's chair. At that point, Aphrodite's babies forgot their young manners. The smell of cheese and nuts proved too great a temptation.

"Stay the course, old girl," Millicent heard her father say. "They are coming up your skirts."

Sure enough, Millicent bent over to see the wee mice using her mother's skirts as a bridge to gain access to the dinner table.

"Lord Fen!" Millicent screamed. "I'll get the cat, you get the mice. "Now! Hurry!" Millicent lost her decorum completely.

Lord Maclaevane somehow managed to capture two of the mice. Before Fen ran the length of the table, Millicent's father caught one.

"Don't squeeze too hard, Father. You will crush it and it's Fen's pet."

"Nonsense, my dear," her mother said. "He's an old hand with baby mice. You forgot that when you were about three years of age, you adopted a family of mice with the help of your brothers. Evil boys."

"Good work, Your Grace," Lord Maclaevane said.

"Not at all, my boy. Glad to help. Reminds me of my younger days, after I found I had a daughter in the fall of my years. I should have been bouncing grandchildren on my knee and my wife presents me with a daughter."

Lord Fen caught the remaining mice, but most of the guests still milled about in the hall, evidently afraid to come back. "I'll fetch my bagpipes," Fen shouted and a joyous cry went up.

"Mulled wine and coconut cakes in the great hall," the countess announced.

Millicent didn't need to add another word. The crowd dissipated leaving her alone with her parents.

"Wonderful dinner, my dear," said her mother. "I couldn't have handled it better."

"Thank you, I have learned from the best."

"Your Grace, may I have a private word with you?" Lord Maclaevane said. Millicent's heart leaped in her chest.

"I've heard those words often enough," Millicent's father said. "What makes you think a highlander is good enough for my daughter? My exceedingly rich daughter, I might add."

"I fell in love with a penniless woman, or so I believed. A woman with spirit and fire, of that I had no doubt. One who was not afraid to speak her mind, save one occasion. I had no idea Lady Mary was Lady Millicent. The same woman my good friend Lord Andrew asked me to seek out."

"You know my brother?" Millicent asked.

"Later, your father wants an explanation at the moment, not a revelation of how I know your brother," Lord Maclaevane reminder her.

"It's true, Father. I lied to Lord Maclaevane. I pretended to be cousin Mary. He asked for my hand thinking I had no father to ask for permission."

"My publisher let his part in this deception slip," Millicent's mother said. "We had to threaten to have him imprisoned before he admitted to sending you away."

"It was my idea," Millicent told everyone, only to have three heads shaking at her declaration.

"Who told you I was seeking a governess?" Lord Maclaevane asked.

"Who made your traveling plans?" her mother asked.

"Who first suggested the highlands of Scotland?" her father questioned.

"Mother's publisher," Millicent admitted.

Her father rubbed his chin. "What was your answer to Lord McDougal's proposal?"

"I said yes. I immediately said yes. But then he took his proposal back."

Lord Maclaevane took her hand. "You wounded me when you revealed your true identity. At first, I just reacted. You took me by surprise. After my initial response, I found myself backed into a corner of my own making. The countess told me how you came to my home, but even before I knew the truth of how you came to the highlands I still wanted you as my wife. Yet, if I spoke too soon you may have believed I was motivated by your dowry."

Millicent squeezed his hand. "Is that why you kept me on tenterhooks?"

"That and the fact I had not spoken to your father. How could I tell you I love you without first asking his permission?"

"You love me?"

"It is *you* who have not said anything of love," Lord Maclaevane reminded her.

"I have never been in love," Millicent said. "I didn't understand the emotions warring inside me. Now, I can give them a name. From the moment you asked for my hand, I knew. I love you."

"Do you want to wed the highlander?" Millicent's father asked.

"Yes, I do."

"A highlander?" her father repeated. "You have all of London beating down my door, but you choose to come to Scotland?"

"Not *a* highlander, Father. Lord McDougal is *my* highlander."

Even with the banns posted it took three weeks to pull the wedding together.

"I am so proud of you, my daughter," Millicent's mother said as they stood in the rear of the chapel before her father was to lead her down the aisle.

"Are you certain? Have I fallen short?"

"My sweet girl, when did I ever have a single cross word for you?"

Millicent didn't want her mother taking any responsibility for her misbehavior. "Never! You are too well-mannered to be cross with me."

Her mother hugged her close. "It had nothing to do with manners. I dared not say a cross word because you were harder on yourself than I ever could have been, even if I had wanted. And I certainly did not."

Millicent couldn't believe her ears. All these years she was certain she had let her mother down.

"Once again you have put your brothers to shame. Here you are, the last of my children to be born and the first to marry. It would serve them right if they waited too long and you have the male heir to the dukedom."

"Poor child that."

Her mother laughed. "Only you, my Millicent. Now go take hold of your father's hand. You have the most handsome man in all of Scotland waiting at the altar for you."

"Mother!"

"Remember your manners, Millicent. Don't keep your dashing highlander waiting. Take a close look at his face. He is worried you will bolt at the last minute, poor boy. He is besotted, as the countess would say."

Millicent looked down the aisle and into his eyes as she reached for her father's hand. It was true. Her highlander loved her with a love as fierce and steady as the mountains over Loch Droma.

She took a step forward and began a very mannerly march toward heaven with her highlander.